INVASION AFTER

Ashley Felts

Dedication

I would like to dedicate this book to my amazing husband, Patrick, and my cousin and friend, Sarah Beth, and my dad, Keith, for all their help

Table of Contents

About the Author

Ashley is a Meteorology major, but quickly decided after college that writing was her passion with stories and ideas coming easily to her. She can't wait for people to read her work and hopes everyone enjoys the journey she will take you on. With a million ideas to get on paper, it's only a matter of time before one of them is a hit.

Chapter One

"I fucking hate graduations," I hissed as I started to light a cigarette.

"When did you start smoking, Sayrah?" Talents whispered. "And anyway, you can't smoke those here. We're in the middle of a crowd. Come on, we are going to get in trouble."

"Who cares," I said at a volume that made a few people look. I caught the eye of a judgy woman a few seats over. I stuck my tongue out at her and said out loud, "Can I help you?" The lady scoffed and turned away while I reluctantly put my cigarette back in the pack. "Fine," I said begrudgingly with a sigh. "I won't smoke." As much as I loved making Talents upset, I decided to be nice. I looked him in the eyes and for a split second, I took off my cloaking of my eyes, which turned blood red, and winked at him. His eyes widened and he gave me a little smack on my shoulder. I grinned and changed them back to the fake, generic green color.

But my smile didn't last long. I remembered I wasn't happy. Today was not a happy day. Talents and I hadn't seen our mother in three years. She had wanted some space for a reason she had kept to herself, but our lives are so long that a few Earth years didn't make much of a difference. We occasionally kept in contact with a few meetings on our ship orbiting Earth's moon, but she had only recently told us the big news: she was engaged. I had mixed emotions; however, they were all bad.

So many things were wrong with her marrying a human. First, she would outlive him for many years. How was she supposed to explain looking like a thirty-year-old for the rest of his life? Our mother's solution was simple: she was going to tell her fiancé and show her true self to him. She was going to tell him she was a different alien species called a Link and try to convince him to come live with her on our planet, Maltina.

But it was just so weird! Humans only live a hundred years, if they are lucky. I had never considered being with a species that has such a short life. Of course, I haven't really ever considered being with anyone, Link, or any other species. Accept Ogy… But I didn't wanna think about him. It hurt too much.

Still, it just didn't make sense. I felt like she was keeping something from us, but I couldn't put my finger on what it was. Mother was good at keeping secrets. She also liked her space. She loved Talents and me, but she didn't always want to spend time with us, which was a topic of disagreement. I wanted to spend all my time with Mother, so it hurt a little that she was so keen on space every few hundred years.

I looked at Talents. It was always weird when we were out in public together because we had to have our cloak on. If not, all the humans would see we have purple skin, and that wouldn't settle well.

Talents slapped my arm to wake me from my daydreaming and stood up violently as he started clapping. I rolled my eyes, stood up, and cheered for my mother as she crossed the stage to receive her diploma. It all felt pointless. After today, or soon after, depending on how Mother's fiancé reacted to the news of her being an alien, we would be heading back to Maltina. We may not come back to Earth for a hundred years. What was she going to do with her degree? It would just be a memento of her time here on Earth as it rested in her bungalow on our planet.

What I was about to realize was that she wasn't even going to have her diploma on Maltina because Earth didn't have much time left.

Then, Talents and I both felt our communicators vibrate in our pockets. We gave each other a worried look. It was only supposed to do that in an emergency. But then we looked up at the sky and knew something bad was about to happen.

***

In a mere few moments, I would be holding my degree and would finally be on my way to becoming an actor. I could practically taste the diploma and feel the leather binding it was encased in. The ceremony was taking place in the main quad of the college campus. It was surrounded by gray stone buildings, all about four stories in height. The grass had been freshly cut the day before, and the smell of earthiness still filled the air.

I awaited hearing my name: Norman Calloway. My name was actually Norman, but I preferred Knor. It had a better sound to it and made me feel a little more ambiguous and unique. When I was younger, I had considered changing it to Thor, but I thought maybe it was a little too cheesy and worried it wouldn't catch on.

Unfortunately, what I didn't know was everything was about to change, and what people called me wouldn't matter.

I stared at the faculty and staff who sat on a makeshift stage on the library terrace. Slowly, one row at a time, the graduating class would stand, then line up at the stage and walk across to receive their degree. I sat nervously in my fold-up metal chair. I had worked so hard for that degree, although it wasn't my first one.

Five years ago, during my first graduation, I received a degree in political science. At that point, I had a thriving desire to change the world. I hoped to be the second Black male president of the United States. I wanted to be in charge, help people, and make my country a more respectable place to call home. Sadly, the further along I got into the degree, the more I knew it wasn't my calling. The passion just disappeared for whatever reason. But that was also when I realized it was hard to switch majors once the upper-level core classes had been completed. So I stuck it through and listened to the parroted advice people had given: "Having a degree on your resume is better than not having a degree."

It turned out to be unwise advice. I couldn't perform well in the few jobs I had in political science. I just didn't have the heart for it anymore.

So, at twenty-four, after failing at multiple political assistant positions, I decided to get a second degree. This time, however, I chose theater. It was a degree everyone thought was far more useless than my political science degree, but no one's opinion mattered to me. Ever since I was ten, I have participated in many community theater productions. They all brought me so much joy. The elation I felt being on stage was indescribable. I loved everything about it—being a different character, the clothes, being in front of an audience. All of it put me in a state of excitement. I couldn't think of anything that made me happier, except maybe being with my fiancée.

But at twenty-seven, I was finally achieving my goal. I had no idea what I was going to do with my new degree—maybe apply to Julliard or move to California to pursue an acting career—but I had never been more content in my choice to become an actor. And, better yet, I met my future wife in the program. I looked up proudly at the stage as she walked across and received her degree. Her smile melted my heart.

But then something strange happened.

As she stepped off the stage, she stopped right before her aisle and examined the crowd. I stopped clapping, noticing the silence. It was awkward and almost painfully quiet, but then everyone started gazing up at the sky.

The graduation ceremony ceased as a foreign object became visible in the atmosphere. It appeared peeking down through the barrier of gray, low-lying stratus clouds that had been shielding the ceremony from the sun. The thick cotton web above had promised rain but had failed to produce any so far. That had allowed the graduation to continue uninterrupted. Until now.

We were all mesmerized by the metal cube floating above us. It was high up in the sky but large enough to see there were no blinking lights or sounds coming from the still object. Instead, it hovered, stationary, as the dusty clouds seeped around its ridged edges. It wasn't until an opening silently appeared at its base that people started to react.

Some let out a slight gasp, while others pulled out their phones to record the event. A decent amount of people even started running. I didn't watch them to see where they were going; I just looked back up at the sky. I was waiting for something. I didn't know what exactly, but I assumed something would happen. Instead, a small gust of wind blew across the quad. My graduation cap quickly flew off. I reached up instinctually to grab it, but it disappeared into a sea of caps blowing in the wind. My graduation gown was mildly off-kilter and clung close to my body.

I should have been grateful for the light wind. It dried up the layer of sweat that had formed from sitting in the humid late-spring air. The clouds had blocked the sun but didn't protect us from the heat.

I couldn't take my eyes off the sky. If I had, I would have missed the sudden appearance of the other objects hidden behind the clouds.

One by one, dull metal cubes broke through the gray cloud barrier. They began to form a grid pattern in the shallow atmosphere. Each cube appeared to be about the size of a football field, although they were high up, so it was hard to tell their actual size. They were positioned almost directly next to each other. Each one appeared and then opened its hatch at the base, causing the light wind near the surface to increase in speed and ferocity.

Finally, I blinked, my eyes stinging and watering from the increasingly erratic wind. A small tear fell down my face. It rolled slowly and finally dripped off my cheek. I was finally waking up from my stupor and shock. My heart began to quicken its pace; my chest tightened with fear. Everyone was panicking and rushing haphazardly across the four-acre area.

The students ran and crashed into one another. They looked desperately for their families, who had been positioned behind the graduating class. Then, rows of friends and family replicated the same frantic motions as they rushed forward to find their loved ones. At the same time, the faculty started running. I finally snapped out of my shocked state, and my brain registered why everyone was running for their lives.

The open quad did not feel safe.

The chaos would have been funny to watch—everyone scurrying around as they tried to run but falling clumsily into each other instead, arms flailing. People making outrageous faces. Unfortunately, the screams of panic and terror weren't funny at all, and they were impossible to drown out.

I'd admit, that my first reaction was the same alarm that had infected the crowd. I wanted to find my family and a safe place to gather my thoughts. However, my family didn't come to the ceremony. It was my second degree and my second graduation. I didn't want to waste my family's time. And I'm glad I hadn't. They were hundreds of miles away, safe from the mass confusion. Well, I hoped they were.

I continued to examine the sky. There was no end to the objects gridded in the clouds. For all I knew, the things were everywhere.

It took a minute, but finally, the expected wave of adrenaline crashed through me. It nearly catapulted me into the same hysteria everyone else was in, but luckily, I caught sight of my fiancée. My sweet, kind fiancée. Just knowing she was there with me calmed my nerves. I suppose it shouldn't have. I should've gotten an alpha-protective feeling toward the woman I loved. If I was honest, she was the strong one in the relationship. I'd be lying if I said I didn't lean on her far more than she leaned on me.

She caught sight of me for a moment but almost instantly returned her gaze to the sky.

The people in the stands had tapered down to about a dozen. Those few who were left shared the same bravery—or maybe the same stupidity. They all recorded the event that was transpiring. My fiancée and I were the only ones not filming the scene.

I waited there for a moment, watching her. She stood alone a couple of rows ahead of me, but she looked odd. She didn't appear scared. She looked angry—like she had a few months ago when she'd almost gotten into a fight with a big guy at a bar because he'd kept putting his hands on her. Her face was fierce then, and she definitely hadn't needed any help taking him. Luckily for him, he'd stopped.

Her lips were pursed, a scowl on her brow. Why did she look so angry?

"Sally!" I shouted. I hoped she could hear me over the increasing roar of the wind.

She glanced quickly in my direction. Even her inch-long, sand-colored hair was being tousled by the strong gusts. Her delicate hazel eyes caught mine, and I noticed her expression instantly changed. She wasn't angry anymore. Her eyes were wide and longing, and she appeared sad.

She looked up once more at the ominous objects and then shook her head.

We quickly made our way toward each other.

"This is crazy!" I yelled through the wind as we reached each other's side. I leaned in for a comforting hug from the woman I loved, but she tensed up, pushed me back, and stared up at the sky. It reminded me of my grandparents' rigid, nonexistent affection. But

Sally was normally very affectionate. I didn't think she had ever pushed me away.

She barely acknowledged I was beside her. She shook her head. I couldn't hear her well but could read her lips. "This is bad," she said over and over again.

"Maybe we should go inside?" I suggested.

The wind made it hard to think, and I longed for the false comfort of four walls. I felt like I did when a hurricane came through my town when I was a kid. The walls of my home surrounding me were comforting, but, as an adult, I know I was incredibly lucky to have survived.

It was funny how no one actually knew what those objects were, but our instant reaction was fear. For all we knew, the wind would soon stop, and candy would drop down on everyone below. Unfortunately, everyone's instincts were correct. A sugar high was not in our near future.

Sally looked at me, now giving me her full attention. The intensity of her stare stung. At first, I couldn't quite read her expression. She seemed sad and angry and maybe a little bit confused. But then she scanned my face as if looking for the answers there. Finally, she settled on an even more painful expression: pity. Like a parent would look at a child who didn't yet understand the meaning of death.

"Hiding won't help," she insisted as she glared at me.

"How do you know?"

I wondered why she was being so pessimistic. It wasn't like her. She normally had a positive attitude, even in bad situations. Maybe the craziness was just too much for her positive personality.

My unsettled graduation gown made it hard to think. It burned as it thrashed at my skin in the strong wind. Everything suddenly turned blue as my gown covered my face. Before I had a chance to move it, a fold-up chair came crashing into me, and I fell to the ground. I grunted as the gown magically moved and allowed me to face plant into the dirt. I tasted the bitter grass and a little blood where my lower lip had just busted. I glanced up for a moment while my clothes continued to whip around. The chairs started to move about. We needed to get out of the wind. I didn't want to die from a metal folding chair accident.

"Let's at least get out from the open," I insisted as I stood up.

Sally didn't move or even respond to what I'd said. I wasn't certain if she had even heard me. I realized while I was focused on standing up and avoiding rogue chairs, Sally had put on some strange glasses. And she was holding what looked like a see-through tablet.

"What is that?" I asked loudly, even more confused and very surprised by her new accessories. I reached out to touch them and she swatted my arm away. I recoiled in disbelief. Why was she being so cold?

She looked at me for just a moment, opened her mouth as if to speak, but all she settled on was, "I'm sorry," and continued ignoring me as she looked at her tablet.

The glasses had a purple tint to them, and they hugged close to her eyes. There was no strap or extension holding them on. They gently rested on her high cheekbones and somehow stayed secure through the gusts of wind. I could see her eyes through the lenses. They flicked quickly back and forth, focused on something. I looked in the direction she was staring, yet saw nothing but uninteresting trees and the side of a building. Her eyes jutted back and forth as if she was reading something. Then it hit me—the only explanation I had was that information was appearing within the frames. I wondered if it was a computer screen.

"What kind of glasses are those?" I asked through the wind. But once again, she didn't answer. She just continued to look back and forth between the glasses and the tablet.

I let out a short laugh under my breath as I thought of how weird it would be if Sally had some advanced technology I didn't know about. Then I glanced at the dark sky filled with those strange gray masses. Never mind. It wouldn't be that weird.

As I focused more closely on the tablet, I saw it was more like a panel of glass. It didn't appear to have any hidden circuits or power supply, but there was definitely information popping up on the screen that she was interacting with. I examined it closely to see if I could figure out what she was doing, but nothing on the screen made sense. There weren't words or numbers but strange squiggles. At least, to me, they looked like little squiggles. If she had been messing with her smartphone, I would have thought it was some strange new game or app, although I was pretty sure it was more complicated than a game. She didn't quite get such a serious face when she was playing Flappy Bird.

She kept looking up at the sky, tapping a few things on the screen, then looking up again as if searching for something specific. My heart dropped. It appeared as if she knew what was going on.

"Come on," she shouted harshly. "Where are you?"

"Sally?" I said hesitantly. My throat caught as I said her name. As I became more scared, the pinch of salted tears prickled in my eyes. The one person who I could turn to for security and comfort in a situation like that was instead making everything worse. She felt so distant even though she stood right next to me. As I shook my head and took a deep breath to center myself, I wondered again if she knew what was going on.

"Damnit!" she cursed loudly.

She placed her hands onto what looked like very sharp corners of the glass screen, the razor edges pressing directly into the palms of her hands. I shouted, "Hey! Be careful," thinking she was about to impale her hands on the fresh glass. But instead, as she pushed in, the glass simply disappeared. And once the screen vanished, the glasses that rested on her face disappeared like a thin sheet of sugar falling into the water.

"What's going on?" I whispered, my voice catching again as I tried to hold back my fear and not cry. I was surprised when she actually looked at me this time. I didn't expect her to acknowledge me since she'd been ignoring me until then. As she stared deeply at me, my heart began to beat faster. Her stare was not comforting. It was determined and intense.

It scared me.

She continued to look directly into my eyes. Even my soul felt uncomfortable as her gaze bore into me. I could tell she had a lot she suddenly wanted to say. It was the look people in movies get right before they think they are going to die. I felt sure that we were going to be destroyed, and all I wanted was to hold her close for the last moments of our lives. But before I could reach for her, she spoke.

"Knor, you know I love you, right?" she asked as her breathing began to quicken. She reached out and finally held my hand. I paused for a moment before becoming almost angry. She had been so mean, and then, she wanted to talk about love.

"What?!" I shouted, immediately thrown out of my romantic stupor. "Why are you asking me that? Of course, I love you." I grunted at her. "What's going on?" I demanded, her uncomfortable stare almost sending me over the edge.

She quickly glanced up at the sky once more and then opened her mouth, as if about to speak. But then, from behind her, two purple-skinned figures appeared.

Chapter Two

Talents and I stared at each other for a moment and looked up at the sky. There they were. The Zyeenan ships. They had found us. But how? I looked at Mother. She was standing next to the stairs of the library focused on the sky. She looked concerned, as she should.

Talents and I both reached for our communicators and opened our tablets. Our glasses appeared over our eyes and we began processing the information that showed up on the screen.

It didn't take long for Talents to speak up. "It's not a recognizance mission," he said.

"They are everywhere," I whispered, still in shock, as the other ships began to appear.

Zyeens have a few reasons why they would show themselves to an unexpecting species. For one, they may be trying to make allies. Humans could be vicious and Zyeens were definitely vicious, so maybe they thought with humans' advancing technology, they would be good allies. However, if that were the case, they would have only sent one ship, not a whole fleet. But as more and more ships began to appear in the sky, Talents and I knew it wasn't to become allies.

Another reason they could be here was to take the planet's resources. Zyeens were like pirates in that sense. They would destroy unsuspecting planets and steal whatever metals or resources they desired.

But then there was the reason that haunted Talents and me. They had come for us. Zyeens held a grudge against Links. They considered us a pest of a species, which was rich coming from them. But still, they had destroyed our home multiple times. Maltina was simply the name we gave to any planet we terraformed. Which, in this case, was the planet the humans called Venus.

Links were an advanced species with technology beyond many other cultures, but the Zyeens weren't far behind. In a way, we were always running from them. They were like hunters that Links just couldn't shake. All Zyeens wanted was to kill all of the Links, but they hadn't yet succeeded.

And now, here they were. Their ships fill up the skies. I felt a little guilty. They may be here for the planet's resources, but it was a little too suspicious that Mother, Talents, and I were here just as the Zyeens arrived. Which meant they were probably here because of us. They were here to kill us. And by the looks of it, they were going to destroy everything.

I looked at my tablet and confirmed they were surrounding the whole planet. Earth was about to be destroyed. And although I had no alliance with it or even cared for any human on it, I did feel guilty. Humans were about to be wiped out. And it was probably our fault.

I looked at Talents at the same time he glanced at me. "We need to go to Mother," I said. Talents nodded and we clicked off our cloak and made our way to her side.

***

With everything going on, I didn't think I could possibly be any more afraid. The wind continued to gust, UFOs floated motionlessly in the sky, and most surprising of all, my fiancée appeared to have at least some understanding of what was going on.

Yet, somehow, in the midst of all of the unexplainable chaos, I still managed a gasp when the two purple figures ran up behind Sally. "Look out!" I shouted as I grabbed Sally and moved her toward me.

"What are you doing?" Sally hissed. She was clearly on edge and was momentarily taken aback by the sudden movement. I continued to stare at the figures.

"Behind you!"

I held tight to Sally as she looked up at me. I was about to start running and pull her along when Sally finally turned around to see what I'd not been able to take my eyes off of. But, to my surprise, instead of looking scared, she immediately looked relieved to see the pair of purple beings.

"There you are," she stated, completely turning away from me. I still held tight to her, but she quickly pulled away.

"No!" I demanded as I reached for her again, trying to protect her from the purple beings. "We need to run!"

"No," she said calmly as she grabbed my hand that held firmly to her arm and removed my grip with strength she didn't normally possess. "They're okay."

I looked back and forth at her and the violet beings for a moment. They did look like humans. Just with different colored skin and eyes. The purple beings were both young-looking. If I had to guess, I'd say late teens. The more I stared at them, the clearer their clothes and facial features became. I could see one figure was a tall woman, at least five foot ten. Her skin was a dark purple, and her hair was curly, long, and a deep, dark red, almost like fresh blood. Her features and stoic demeanor were definitely admirable, although still very off-putting. She was beautiful. Her eyes, which were blood-red like her hair, looked closely at Sally.

The guy, on the other hand—well, I wouldn't go as far as to say he was unattractive, but his uniqueness made it difficult to decide. He was, at max, five foot five, and his skin was a strange violet purple. It was almost glowing and electric. But his hair was short and blond, almost yellow. As I looked closer at his eyes, I could see they were actually purple, and he was staring right at me. That wasn't reassuring.

I still wanted to run, but I felt guilty. I didn't want to leave Sally, the woman I deeply loved. But there were floating, ominous objects in the sky, and my fiancée was definitely hiding something. She clearly knew what was going on, and to top it all off, two purple people just showed up. And Sally knew them.

I questioned my sanity.

I thought for a moment that maybe it was a dream. The graduation ceremony hadn't been the most exciting thing in the world. The school had asked some extremely old alumnus to speak to us about the future, but instead, he'd talked mostly about the past (and spoke very slowly). It wasn't a complete stretch to think I may have fallen asleep while it was happening. Or maybe I had a brain tumor deep in my skull. I'd heard those were known for creating intense and realistic hallucinations. Maybe it was some terrible delusion a brain tumor had created for me.

Unfortunately, as much as I hoped for a brain tumor, I somehow knew in my heart everything was all really happening. Even though it was the most unbelievable thing I had ever seen, it felt too damn real to be a dream.

***

"Mother, this is bad," I said as I gave Knor a side eye, but looked back at Mother. "What are we supposed to do?"

"We have to get to our ship," Mother said. "They are going to destroy Earth."

"They are charging their weapons," Talents said sternly as he looked at his tablet. "We can't get to the ship because of a signal blocker. They've advanced since the last time we dealt with them." Talents looked up from his screen with fear in his eyes. "What are we supposed to do?"

"We have to stay through the first wave," Mother said seriously.

I shook my head. "There's no way your force field can protect us for long enough," I said desperately. I didn't want Mother to die from using all her energy. Her force field takes a lot of her power. And to protect us from the firestorm that was about to happen would take most if not all of her strength.

"I have to try," Mother said.

I looked over at the pitiful human named Knor. He looked like a lost puppy looking for a home. I didn't want him with us, but I couldn't do anything about it. Maybe I could push him out of the force field right before the destruction that was about to happen from the first wave. I sighed. I was stuck with this hitchhiker. But it didn't mean I was going to be nice to him.

Then, the ships began to move.

***

For a short moment, I wondered who Mother was. But the curiosity didn't last long. I was frozen, caught up in fear and confusion, thinking about all the possibilities. However, my fight-or-flight instincts took hold. Flight was the more prominent feeling; I didn't really want to fight the woman I loved. I also definitely didn't want to pick a battle with those two purple people or whatever they were. Thus, flight seemed to be my only option. I wasn't sure where I would run, but I needed to get away. I had to find a calm place to think. All I could hope for was a quiet spot to gather my thoughts.

I started to plan my escape, getting ready to make my move, but Sally was talking to the two purple figures. As much as I wanted to run, I couldn't leave Sally. And also, I was curious about what they were saying.

I heard a few jumbled sentences about destruction and force fields and ships, but they also seemed to be under the impression that we were stuck and had to deal with something called "the first wave," whatever that meant. I grabbed Sally's shoulder and tried to get her to look at me. "We have to get out of here!" I said with vigor. But the two purple figures and Sally only looked at me for a second, as if I had said something stupid, and continued talking. I was definitely the odd man out. I no longer felt like I belonged at Sally's side.

I didn't know what else to say to Sally, and no one seemed to want to actually go inside a building. I felt guilty, but it was time to go. I kept my eyes on them while I turned. It wasn't until my neck had reached its full range of motion that I took my gaze off them. There was a microsecond that I felt relieved, like somehow getting away from there would make everything okay. Graduation caps and folding chairs crashed around me. But the library across the quad was still and stable. It seemed like a safe place to be away from the wind and out of sight of the metal cubes. It was probably a futile thought; whatever was about to happen, it probably wouldn't help me to be inside the library, but it was the only speck of sanity and hope I had left. And mostly everyone else, even the insane people who were filming, had gone inside. It was just a handful of people: me, Sally, and her two purple friends. We were definitely the crazy ones.

Unfortunately, as I turned away, someone grabbed my hand before I could take another step.

"Knor, stop!" Sally shouted as she held tightly to my hand.

"Let him go," the purple woman said. I heard it, but no one else seemed to be paying her attention. I heard her scoff.

Sally's grip was stronger than usual. My reflex was to pull as hard as I could to get away, but her hold was too firm. I paused for a moment, tension still present between her grip and my arm. The male figure gave me a puzzled stare. I wondered if he wanted me there or not. It didn't seem the purple woman did.

I looked at Sally for a second, then caught the confused and judgmental stares of the purple people and turned away. I was too scared, and there were so many eyes on me. The "flight" feeling intensified.

"I'm going inside," I said as I turned away from her. My eyes closed, and I looked down. I felt shame for wanting to leave, but I could still feel her and the other two people staring at me. It made me want to run away even more.

I pulled hard once again to try and escape her grip, but Sally just held on tighter. I didn't know she was so strong. Anytime we wrestled or play-fought, I was always able to overpower her. But then, even with my adrenaline flowing strong, I couldn't free myself from her unyielding grasp.

I turned toward her and stared at her hand on my arm. I needed to get a better angle so I could free myself from her grip. I reached my other hand to try and pry her from my skin.

"Let go," I quietly ordered; those shameful tears once again began to prick at the corners of my eyes. "Just let me go." But instead of releasing her hold, she caught my other hand with her free one and pulled my whole body close to her.

I stumbled forward, completely surprised by her overwhelming strength and the unexpected motion. I looked at her, my eyes probably wide-and my face dumbfounded. I was sure she could see my tears.

We were very close then, maybe only a few inches apart. She stared deep into me. I couldn't tell if she was waiting for me to talk or if she had something important to say. Her eyes stung me as she stared. I was suddenly angry at her for being dishonest. Even though I didn't even really know what the lie was, with everything happening, I still felt wounded by the woman I loved. She had lied to me and was living some secret life I didn't know about. I was hurt. I thought I knew her so well, but I stood staring at a stranger.

I closed my eyes and tried to look away from her, but she let go of my hands and placed both of her palms on either side of my face, which forced me to look at her. The motion would normally have made me feel uncomfortable; I wasn't an animal or child who needed to be controlled. But for some reason, at that moment, it was okay as I felt her cool hands on my warm cheeks. There was so much love in her eyes—and so much fear. I brought one of my hands up to touch hers as her palms held tightly to my face, those pesky tears trying to release themselves from my eyes.

"I need you to listen to me," Sally said in a calm but authoritative tone. "I know you're scared and confused, but there isn't time to explain everything right now."

"Moth- uh... Tierly?" said the male voice behind Sally.

I glanced at him for a moment and noticed he had on the same strange glasses Sally had been wearing a few moments ago. I looked at the woman and she also had a tablet and glasses.

"Hold on!" Sally barked as she glanced away for just a second, and then returned her eyes to me, her hands still gripping my face.

Tierly? Had Sally responded to that name? And I still didn't know who 'Mother' was.

"I know what's happening," Sally said bluntly. "But we don't have time for questions. If you want to survive, I need you to stay with me. Your cooperation will determine whether you live or die. Hold my hand, and don't let go."

She looked away from me and removed her hands from my face. Then she quickly grabbed hold of my right hand. At first, I thought I would jerk away and run as fast as I could away from her. But it finally hit me when I looked up at the endless metal grid of fear floating above me. As far as I could see, there was no space left in the sky. No clouds, just metal cubes.

There wasn't anywhere I could run to. Hiding somewhere in a building wasn't going to save me from whatever was about to happen.

The fear settled in, and I could no longer move on my own. Fight-

or-flight had disappeared, and I was useless, exhausted, and compliant. For a moment, things became blurry. I stood where I was, swaying back and forth. I heard mumbles and muffled gusts of wind, but I couldn't make out anything anyone was saying. I looked up and saw blurred visions of foreign objects floating above. I blinked and tried to clear my distorted view. But instead, the world went black for a moment. I felt pressure on one side of my body, and a moment later, I could feel the cool grass between my fingers.

My body jolted twice, which I think was Sally shaking me; my ears ached with the loud sounds of her screaming at me. Then there was pressure on my face, which stung and was so strong my head slung to the side. I heard an unfamiliar female voice say again, "Just leave him." I assumed it was the dark purple-skinned woman. I could hear the anger, but also urgency in her voice.

I felt burning on one side of my face and cool grass on the other. I quickly became aware of my surroundings. The blurry vision was gone and I could hear again. I was on the ground. Sally held my shoulders and looked at me with concern. The female behind her gave a slight disapproving glance but quickly focused back on her strange, clear tablet. She didn't seem interested in my presence. The man was looking at me, but as I caught his eyes, he gave me a pitiful smile. Once again, someone was looking at me as if I were a child.

I looked toward Sally. Above her, I could see the metal objects hovering. Then the metal squares started to spin.

"They're moving," I said, staring up at them.

Sally's eyes widened. She turned to see the sky for herself.

The female being shouted over the wind, "They're about to fire the first wave!" Orange light shined from the small hole at the base of all the metal objects. It was a beautiful color, much like looking at the sun. The light didn't hurt my eyes, but it was probably going to cause something worse than skin cancer.

Sally stood up and continued to look at the sky. Both the male and female strangers moved in close and crouched near her legs. It was a weird gesture to see. I didn't understand what they were doing. I lay there confused until the female purple person, finally begrudgingly acknowledged that I was there and quickly grabbed my arm. She pulled me right next to her. I resisted the suddenness of the whole action, so instead of moving into the same crouched position as the other two, I landed face-first on the ground, again. The woman scoffed.

I lifted my head up quickly and took a deep breath. The impact had knocked the wind out of me, and I tasted sour dirt. I tried to breathe and spit the grass out of my mouth all at once. However, before I caught my breath, the woman anchored her hand under my armpit and successfully pulled me toward her.

"Do you wanna lose your feet?" she asked sarcastically as she pulled me in, but quickly tossed my arm away.

I didn't know what she meant, so I wasn't sure how to respond, and I wasn't thinking clearly. But no matter what was about to happen, she was correct that I didn't want to lose my feet. So I stayed close to this strange woman, huddled next to Sally's feet.

I felt awkward beside Sally's legs in the same squatted state as the other two people. I was about to ask what we were doing when I noticed a blue glow out of the corner of my eye. A light started to flash, and I turned to see what was happening. I expected to see a strobe light or something like that, but instead, I saw Sally's hands flashing with electricity. She held her hands together, palms flat, while the spikes of electricity made their way from her hands down into her arms. Suddenly she was glowing from her shoulders through her arms and electricity jolted from her hands.

Her hands were close to my head, and I made a motion to move away, but the woman beside me grabbed on tight.

"Don't move," she ordered with an irritated look on her face.

The woman scared me a little. Well, actually, she scared me a lot, but I decided she knew more than I did, so I should probably listen to her. I kept my body still but allowed my gaze to once again find Sally's electric hands. It was incredible to see, even though I was terrified I was going to get shocked.

I examined her face. Sally looked calm, and her eyes were closed. I wondered if maybe she was a witch, but I decided against that since she wasn't saying anything. It was only a guess, but I assumed if witches were real, they would have to say something for their magic to work. It was probably a dumb assumption.

Without any words, Sally maintained her stoic face while the speed and quantity of the electricity increased. Her friends looked surprisingly calm as the energy flowed, but the tension increased in my body as the electric current flashed closer and closer to my face. I wondered if my eyebrows would be singed off before or after I was electrocuted to death. Then in a quick, methodic motion, Sally opened her eyes and lifted one arm, stretching it as far as she could above her head. Her fingers expanded, and as they did, the electricity rushed up her arm, and a bright blue light escaped from her fingertips.

I thought the light was going to shoot up into the sky. Instead, it expanded into an elongated dome shape, extending just beyond where the other two people and I crouched; I finally understood why the woman had pulled me in so close. Who knew what that electric light could have done to me?

As the light shaped itself around us, Sally's other hand stretched downward, and she extended that arm straight with her palm facing toward the ground. There was another bright flash. A faint soft light appeared from the ground up through Sally's hand and connected from her other hand to the top of the dome. The light suddenly surrounded us and turned into a nearly translucent blue tint. That, unfortunately, allowed us to see the unimaginable devastation that happened next.

Chapter Three

I grabbed at this man-child as Mother wrapped us in her shield and pulled him close to her legs. "Do you wanna lose your feet?" I asked coldly. I felt like washing my hands after I had touched him. He was exceptionally sweaty. I took a deep breath. *Mother loves this man,* I thought to myself. But it didn't really help. Mother had spent three years getting to know *this* man. In the few moments I had been with him, he had done nothing to impress me. He had passed out and looked like a dying puppy.

I took another deep breath as I pretended to glance away. *Mother loves this man,* I thought again. I don't know why I kept thinking about it. It didn't make me like him any more than I did.

He didn't look like much. I tried to stare at him inconspicuously. He was probably six feet tall with dark skin and short curly hair cut close to his head. He was clean-shaven and had ripped his graduation gown off with the cap being long gone because of the wind. He had on a long-sleeved button-up pink and blue striped shirt with brown slacks. I thought for a moment that he was handsome, but I quickly let that thought go. He was still a man-child in my mind. Who passes out at a time like this? Is he a swooning woman from the 1800s?

I looked at Talents. He was fixed on his tablet. This man, known as Knor, just sat staring out into the quad. I wondered what he was looking at but didn't press the matter. I did have a small urge to talk to him. I wanted to know what he thought of all this. My home had been destroyed three times by the Zyeens. We were always refugees, looking for a new home, which we had found, and we had been there for a while now... But we always called it Maltina, after Mother's mother. Humans called it Venus, but I liked our name better.

I wondered, in the brief seconds we rested by Mother's legs, how the Zyeens had found us. We hadn't received any transmission from Maltina. Had they been destroyed? Or did they find us because we were vulnerable on Earth? Talents and I were notoriously bad about removing our cloak when we were home. I had thought the Zyeens may have finally given up on wiping out the Links after failing so many times to destroy us all. Because what would be the odds that they would attack Earth while we were visiting? Out of all the planets in the universe, what did Earth have that other unoccupied planets didn't?

I knew the answer. It was us. We were the ones they were after.

***

As I and the three others rested fixed in the translucent blue bubble, I caught the eyes of a young woman near the green stone library building about thirty feet away. She had been in my history class. I hadn't wanted to take it, but it was required to graduate. History wasn't really my "thing," so I had kept to myself and hoped it would go by quickly. I didn't know this woman's name, but I knew her face. She presented a beautiful report on the African-American women from the space program in the 1960s. It was a part of history I had never heard of before, and she'd told it more like a story than a history report.

We continued to lock eyes. I wondered if she recognized me. I mustered up a hesitant smile. She was pretty far away, but I was almost certain she gave me a bewildered smile as she scanned the blue light that surrounded me.

It was then that the light on her face began to change. Instead of the dim gray cloudy day, the strange orange light coming from the objects above lit up her skin and the air around her. She and I both glanced away from each other to get a good look at the source. The bright, sun-colored glow emanating from the base of the objects overhead no longer looked like individual lights coming from each square. Instead, they all shone so intensely that the sky was nothing but a layer of deep, orange light. It intensified so quickly and brightly that I felt as if I was surrounded by fire. Even the blue sphere that surrounded us couldn't keep out the brilliance and warmth from the glare. It was so strong that my eyes closed. I feared the fire would kill us. The heat within the blue orb increased. I could feel the temperature rising on my skin, and I was sure in a few moments I was going to be set aflame and burned to death.

The sound of the gusting wind increased while my eyes were closed, and it felt like standing outside during a hurricane. But it was a fire hurricane.

Suddenly, the heat vanished, and I heard no more wind. I hesitantly opened my eyes, glad the bright light had disappeared—but the relief didn't last very long.

Sally broke her locked position, her arms dropping heavily to her sides. She fell to the ground on one knee and closed her eyes. The blue light around us disappeared, and I immediately couldn't see anything. Unable to catch my breath, I coughed incessantly. Huge clouds of smoke filled the air. The sky was covered with black, and the foreign objects were no longer in sight. Only small fires left by the flash allowed us to vaguely see through the dense clouds. All I could see was a small circle of bright green grass that had been underneath the blue dome that had surrounded us. I took in a deep breath, unsure if I would scream or hyperventilate—or even both. Instead, the thick smoky air continued to choke me. I couldn't breathe and began to panic. My throat felt like it was closing, and once again, I feared for my life. The air coming into my lungs felt like lava and nails.

Without warning, I felt two gentle hands being placed on my back and chest. However, the suddenness of the touch and the terror I was experiencing caused me to flail as I fought for air. Two arms wrapped around me, but I still struggled to get away.

"Calm down!" Sally said in a stern tone. "You're panicking. Take a deep breath. The smoke is clearing. You can breathe, just calm down."

I squirmed and twisted hard in her arms, but her tight grip made it impossible to escape. At first, her tight arms felt like a snake coiling around me. I felt more trapped than safe and secure. But eventually, her strong and encompassing embrace caused my nerves to slowly calm down. I took in slow breaths of air and fought hard to relax my tightening throat. I was determined not to die from smoke inhalation.

After a few long moments, the pain in my throat began to fade. I was no longer breathing in glass and fire. My breath became more normal, aside from some coughing. But I couldn't quite get my heart rate to go down.

As I looked around the wind picked up a little and the smoke began to vanish slowly. I entered a state of shock and horror, unable to move from my spot on the ground. I blinked a few times. I couldn't believe it. I felt like I was in the wake of a wildfire; destruction and chaos surrounded me. The once-sturdy buildings were all worthless and crumbled to the ground. Some were partially burned, some still on fire. The grass was all gone. Only scorched, smoking, black earth remained. I could see the trees behind the buildings. Most of them had fallen or were still on fire.

"Everything…" I took a deep breath in as I tried to say what was on my mind. Just the idea of my words made them more terrifying and real. "Everything… Fuck," I whispered. I couldn't speak without the dread welling up inside of me again.

I worked hard to keep my breathing at a normal pace. I wanted to scream and cry and run as fast as I could. My body thought it could sprint to a place that wasn't destroyed, but my mind knew otherwise.

"It's all gone," I managed to whisper, my voice cracking as I fought back tears. I realized quickly that I had a big decision to make: run or trust the three people around me. They all felt like strangers, even the woman I had planned to spend the rest of my life with. I tried to think logically. Obviously, those three had an idea of what was happening, and knowing anything was more than I had. Also, where was I even supposed to go? I had no idea if there was anywhere else to hide.

I decided the only logical thing to do was to trust the three strangers.

I was pretty sure I was making the most pitiful face anyone in the universe had ever made: that wide, teary-eyed anime look. I'm sure I would have gotten a treat if I were a dog begging for food. I could tell I looked pathetic by the way Sally was eyeing me. Her pity made me uncomfortable, but I had decided to trust them, so I looked up at her and asked, "What do we do?"

She let out a heavy sigh. "Knor…" she started. She held one of my hands with hers and placed the other on my shoulder.

She was about to speak again when we heard screams. I tensed up, and my eyes widened even more; people were alive! I thought they were all dead from the blast. Faint moans and screams came from all around us. Instinctually, I wanted to help, but Sally held on to me tightly.

"Let me go!" I screamed at her. "We have to help these people!" God, she was strong.

"Knor!" she said again. This time, she was more forceful as she attempted to regain my attention. "We can't help them," she insisted.

I looked at her, shocked by her indifference to the people I could hear suffering around me. Their distant cries stung my ears. She kept glancing nervously up at the sky.

"What are you talking about?" I yelled. "These people are hurt! We have to help them." Just as I spoke, I looked over to where I had seen the woman. I thought the smoke would be too thick to see her, but then an eerie calm breeze blew in a perfectly straight line and revealed my poor friend. She was lying face down, arms spread wide, and I could see she was still on fire. Her dark chard skin drilled holes in my subconscious.

I moved toward the woman again, but Sally held tight. Her grip squeezed around me even more, and she pulled me so close I could feel the warmth of her breath as she spoke. "No," she said sternly. "We don't have time… And there isn't room."

"There isn't any room?" I asked, frustrated by the confusion I felt and the tight clutch she had on me.

"Tierly," once again said the strange purple man who was with us. "We need to go. There's a break in the signal about a mile away. We're going to have to run there. Phase Two could begin at any moment."

Phase Two? My head was spinning. The confusion, the suffering around me, and the mix of emotions I felt—it was all too much. I felt pathetic. Nothing around me was in my control.

Even as I thought this, Sally grabbed at my hand then forcefully said, "We have to run!" and began pulling me. I followed willingly in whatever direction she decided. I was done. I couldn't process what was going on anymore. I was like a limp, cooked noodle; throw me against a wall, and I would stick. I was *done*.

I followed blankly and obediently as we ran around the destroyed buildings, ignored the few suffering people around us, and crossed jagged, crumbled streets. We made our way into what used to be the wooded area a few hundred yards from the quad. Only thick, charred trees remained. Many had fallen, and we quickly leaped over them. I followed blindly, tripping over trees and trying to stay away from the small fires everywhere.

I was unfocused. My eyes wandered around, slowly taking in the destruction, when Sally suddenly stopped and clapped her hands to catch my attention.

"Hey!" she said firmly. The sudden stop and sound brought me somewhat back to reality. It made me stop my brainless run to look at her. "I need you to focus and stay alert. I know there's a lot going on, but what's about to happen is very important."

I thought we were going to start to run faster, but instead, she continued to look at me.

"We're leaving," she said. Her serious stare gave me chills.

"Oh… kay?" I said, not sure what she was talking about. We had literally just left the quad. Where else could we be going?

"We're going to another planet," she said plainly. The other two people had also stopped. They both were looking through those strange glasses and had their tablets out, but the male being's eyes flicked momentarily in my direction, probably to see how I would respond.

I took a second to look around. Although I didn't even know we could go to another planet or how we would get there, Earth didn't exactly look very habitable anymore. I stared at Sally blankly. The fact was, at that point, she could make me do anything. I was a cooked noodle. She looked serious, so I decided not to tell her my analogy. I was going to say something simple like "Sure" or "That's fine with me," but then I hesitated and took in a sharp breath. What about my family? I gave her a desperate look.

Sally must have read my mind. She instantly responded, "We can't save anyone else. There isn't room on the ship."

Ship? But my confusion didn't matter. The only thing I could think about was all the people I loved. "I can't leave my family," I said. "What if…"

As I was about to state that they could still be alive, faint white lights began to appear through the thick black smoke above us. I was terrified; we were about to be attacked again. I braced myself near Sally and expected the other two to do the same. Instead, the male being shouted abruptly, "Shit, get down!"

We quickly slinked down behind what was left of a crumbled boulder. I looked toward him and saw a faint blinking light coming from the other side of his clear glasses. "Here they come," he said as he pressed on his tablet like Sally had done before and it disappeared between his hands as they clasped together. But he then pulled his hands apart, and a small gun-shaped object appeared. The female being did the same thing, then they both looked up toward the sky.

I was about to follow their lead and look up, but Sally once again caught my attention. "Phase Two is about to begin," she said to me as if I understood.

I remained terrified as I gazed at everything that had already been destroyed. "What does that even mean?" I desperately demanded. My voice even cracked a little, and I could feel a few drops of water slip from my eyes.

"Phase One destroyed most of the environment as well as most life forms and infrastructure of the planet," she began. "Phase Two is the ground attack. They're sending down armed infantry to kill anyone and anything that survived the attack."

I looked away from her for a moment and focused on a suffering person I could hear only a few yards from where we were crouched. Their screams assaulted my ears. All I wanted to do was help them. I didn't understand how anyone had survived the attack in the first place. My mind reeled, and a knot formed in my stomach as I thought of my family.

I shook my head and asked, "Is this happening all over the world?"

"Yes," Sally answered neutrally. "Anyone who's still alive now will only be alive for a few more minutes. There are thousands of infantries on each ship, and they'll be deployed in moments."

I remembered all the objects I had seen above before the smoke covered the sky. I couldn't even count them. I looked up momentarily; beams of white light pushed through the blanket of smoke.

I let my head fall back to rest on the rock we were crouched behind and closed my eyes. I wish I had asked my family to come to my graduation. At least I could have seen them one last time. My eyes burned from the salty tears welling up. I just hoped they weren't suffering.

"Knor?" Sally asked, her voice less aggressive and more empathetic. She was right, though. I needed to focus. I had a big decision to make, and I still only had two options: die on Earth or trust Sally with my life. I wasn't really sure what the second option had in store, but that was just part of the choice.

After a moment, I blinked the tears out of my eyes and looked seriously at Sally. I mustered up some strength and asked, "What do I need to do?"

She gave a hesitant smile. It wasn't really a time for smiles, but she appeared to be happy that I was going to go with her.

"We have to get to our ship," she said sternly, returning to her stoic expression. "They have a signal jammer transmitting over the planet, but there's a small break in it about a mile away. If I have enough energy to teleport us there, then we can connect to the ship and teleport off the planet. The ship is cloaked in orbit around the moon. Once we get there, we'll be safe."

I blinked and stared blankly at her for a few seconds, speechless. What had I just gotten myself into? She was talking about spaceships and teleporting and the moon. I let out a small laugh, took a deep breath, coughed a little as I choked on some smoke, and hesitantly said, "Well… I guess we should get to teleporting?"

The violet-colored male stranger gently placed his hand on my shoulders. I was so overwhelmed by everything going on that I didn't even flinch at his touch. I didn't know who he was. I didn't even know his name. But he gave me a sympathetic smile. I guessed we were about to do that teleportation thing, whatever that entailed.

I noticed Sally's hands were shaped as if she was holding something much like an invisible bowling ball. She seemed intently focused as though trying to make something appear in her hands. Unexpectedly, she tossed her arms in the air in apparent frustration. But quickly, her look of defeat switched to fear. She glanced desperately at the two people beside me. Then she let her arms drop gently to her sides, and she shifted her stare toward me.

"I can't," she said with panic in her voice. I'd never heard her sound so scared. "I used all my energy on the shield. I thought I had enough to teleport us to the break in the signal," she sighed, "but I can't."

She looked down for a moment. She held her hands face up in front of her as she stared at them in disbelief as if they had betrayed her. She looked like she might cry. However, that face only lasted a second. She swiftly lifted her head and once again rested her hands by her side.

"We have to run," she said.

The purple woman spoke up. "But it's a mile away!" she said in defiance as she motioned in the general direction we needed to go. "The ground force will be here at any minute!"

Everyone suddenly looked at me as if I had something important to say. Me—the guy who didn't even know what was happening, let alone how to fix the problem. I honestly didn't even know what the problem was. Maybe Sally was too tired to teleport? She did just save us with a glowing ball of protection. But it still didn't make sense why they were looking to me for an answer. So when they all desperately continued to stare, I just went with what Sally had said. "Maybe we should start running?"

My two new unnamed friends weren't happy with my response, but Sally remained authoritative. "Listen," she said sternly to the three of us, "we have one option: to run. If you don't want to run, fine. Sit here and figure out your own way to get off this dying planet. However, we don't have any more time to talk about this. Knor," she stated as I stared obediently at her. "It's time to go."

Chapter Four

I glared at this man. Why should he get a say in what we do? But I will admit, that guilt was overcoming me. I couldn't stop thinking that the Zyeens had come to destroy… well, had destroyed… this relatively decent planet. And it was probably our fault.

However, mostly I was frustrated. In a matter of minutes, probably seconds, there would be ground troops to kill off the remaining living beings. And Mother couldn't teleport us! For all her powers and abilities, they could be very finicky. It made me think of the human video games where people could play as wizards and had mana, which was like energy money. They only had so much and it had to recharge before you could use it again. That was like Mother. She was powerful and had many abilities but her energy had to recharge, so really I couldn't be mad at her and I understood that she couldn't teleport us. But thinking of running with this halfwit was making me angry.

Knor was suddenly upset about something. I'm not sure what. I wasn't listening. I was focusing on what was about to happen. Mother gave a speech about how we had time to make it to the breaking point, but I was skeptical.

Mother grabbed hold of Knor's hand and began running. I paused for a moment in shock. I didn't like seeing her holding his hand. But I growled under my breath and started to run. But this man! He could barely keep up. Talents and I had to slow our pace because Knor kept falling. Mother kept him going, but barely. We were never going to make it to the break in the signal at this rate.

I was just about to run up to Knor and pick him up because I could run faster holding him then he could stumble, but then they appeared. Four Zyeens soldiers appeared at the base of a teleportation point under their ship. They looked like they knew who we were. Talents and I stood in front of Mother and the man, but put our cloaks back on. It might have been too late and they already knew we were Links, but we tried anyways.

I had turned my tablet, which we called a pendant, into a gun but hid it behind my back. I may not care about this human, but I was ready to destroy these soldiers if they tried to do anything to Mother… or Talents I suppose.

Mother spoke to them in English. She told them to let us pass, but they were suspicious. Our technology was advanced; although we were cloaked and their scanners couldn't tell what species we were, we had survived the first phase unharmed, so of course they were suspicious.

***

I gently nodded my head when Sally said to run, and she simultaneously grabbed my hand. The jerk I felt as she pulled me with her was more forceful than I expected and made my whole body jolt. It was dumb of me to be surprised by her strength. She had overpowered me so many times in only the last few minutes. I should've been used to her power by then.

Still, my body jerked, and we began again to sprint through the woods that were covered with charred fallen trees and branches. Sally continued to run much faster than me. The eager pull from her was not a pleasant feeling; I struggled frantically to keep close to her. I occasionally slipped or stumbled forward, which would slightly pull her back. But my falters did almost nothing to slow her down. She would stop for a moment, then turn around to place her other hand on my shoulder and lift me up. I would feel that shake once more as she held tight to my hand while she barreled through the disheveled forest. The jolt was like an overzealous businessperson's handshake—the way they would vigorously grab a person's hand and yank them toward themselves. No matter how many times they did it, people were always thrown off by the strong tug. I felt like those people every time she pulled me: thrown off and jerked around.

The two other people were close behind. But even with my occasional blunders, they still couldn't keep up with us. I honestly wasn't even sure how I kept her pace. I'd never been a fast runner. My only guess was all the adrenaline running through my system. Of course, I was consistently tripping, so that wasn't exactly "keeping her pace."

The weird thing, or I suppose the *next* weird thing, to happen was a deep humming sound surrounding us. It didn't seem malicious—it was just loud. It sounded similar to a clothes dryer but slightly deeper and definitely more ear-splitting. I wasn't too worried until all three of my companions simultaneously stopped their hasty run. I couldn't tell if the sound of their breathing was that of panic or just exhaustion from running.

It wasn't long until I realized the answer.

"Here they come," the purple woman said in a quiet, breathy voice.

"We have time," Sally said, trying to sound confident.

But I could hear the fear in her voice. I could tell she wanted to be strong, but whether or not we were going to survive the next few minutes was still uncertain.

"We have to keep running," she stated as she grabbed tightly to my hand. "They won't come into the forest until they've cleared the open areas. We only need another couple of minutes, and we'll be able to teleport to the ship. We just need a couple more minutes. We can make it! We just have to run!" She ended her short speech powerfully.

I didn't even know what was going on or what we were even running from or to, but I felt confident we would accomplish whatever we were supposed to. I suddenly felt that familiar tug on my arm again as we started to run. I was slightly more prepared this time to keep up with Sally. Her speech inspired me to think that the situation wasn't as dreadful as it seemed. However, my passion to keep moving came to a swift halt.

In the woods, there was a moment when I couldn't hear the sounds of the suffering people. But all of a sudden, I heard faint, abrupt screams followed by a small sound that resembled the short burst of a car alarm.

Every shriek hit me hard. I wanted to fall to the ground. I wanted to cry. I just wanted to give up. But Sally continued to pull hard to keep me standing and moving. I fought the urge to tell her to let me go. As much as I wanted to be free from her grasp, I also didn't know where to go, and I didn't want to be part of one of those cries.

"One hundred yards straight ahead, and we'll be at the breaking point," shouted the dark violet woman as she ran with us. Her strange glasses were still on.

I felt a faint sense of relief—not enough to smile or relax, just enough to think my chances of dying a horrible death that day were at least a bit lower. To my dismay, I could only enjoy the relief for a moment.

Four strange creatures appeared from out of the sky. They had no parachutes or any type of skydiving gear. They dropped quickly from the bright lights coming from the UFOs above. The lights created a spotlight effect on the ground, and the four beings were within the light. From the harshness of their clothes and stoic stance, they appeared to be soldiers. They were at least seven or eight feet tall. I had never seen anyone that tall in my life. The only person I could think of similar to them was Andre the Giant, who was tall and bulky. But these creatures were even larger than him. The color of their suits was a deep red. In any other situation, I would consider the color beautiful. But right then, the fear of what was underneath distracted me from the beauty that could have been.

The suits were layered like window blinds from the soldier's shoulders to their feet. Only their helmets and shoes were a smooth, form-fitting shape. The material and color were all the same, just structured differently. The soldiers each held what looked like a gun in their hands. They looked like machine guns, but the edges were much smoother.

Sally and the three of us stopped immediately when we saw them. The soldiers were maybe ten feet directly in front of us.

Sally whispered something, but I couldn't tell what she said. It didn't sound like English. It sounded like she was clicking her tongue.

The two purple beings stepped slightly in front of Sally and me while quickly hiding their gun-shaped objects behind their backs. I could only assume from the appearance and the situation they were actual guns. Sally didn't form a gun with her tablet. She didn't even have the tablet out. Instead, she held firmly to my hand.

Then I noticed something strange; our male and female companions were no longer purple. Their skin was the color of a Caucasian person. I didn't know what was more shocking: the large soldiers or the fact that the two people with us were no longer purple but white. Were they chameleons?

But before I could even think to ask, Sally spoke. "Let us pass, and we'll let you live," she exclaimed confidently.

She seemed nervous to me, though. She was holding my hand even firmer than when we were running. I couldn't really blame her. I'd be nervous too. Hell, I was terrified just standing where I was.

The soldier farthest to the right lifted his left hand off his gun and raised it to the mask he wore. On it, he pushed a small button a few times, then returned his hand to his gun. The once-purple man beside me whispered, "That was his translator. He doesn't know what we're saying, but he should now."

I turned to look at him. He strangely shrugged his shoulders and gave me a smile. It was a weird gesture, but being caught up in the moment, I gave him a tiny smile back.

"Let us pass, and we'll let you live," Sally repeated with the same authority.

I guessed they really didn't understand her the first time—their job was to kill, not to talk.

That thought made me feel nauseous.

"No one is to leave this planet alive," declared that same soldier on the far right. His voice was higher than I expected for his size. But I was 90 percent sure it was a guy, assuming that species had gender. I also assumed the translator he turned on also changed his voice because he was speaking English.

"We're almost to our ship," Sally stated. "And we're leaving this planet. It would be wise for you not to try and stop us."

Tension filled the air. The two strangers held tight to the guns, and the four soldiers did the same thing. I tightly gripped Sally's hand, my heart racing. Queasiness and anxiety threatened to overwhelm me.

The soldier on the right turned to his companions. They whispered together for about a minute. The soldiers seemed to relax slightly, but Sally and her friends continued to stay alert, especially when the soldiers finished talking and they turned back to us.

"No," the soldier said. "I don't know how you remained unscathed after the attack. And our scanners cannot identify your species. But no one, human or otherwise, is allowed to leave this planet."

Sally and her friends began to talk without looking at one another in that strange language again. They made sounds like a rural ancient language with clicks and throat sounds. It was beautiful, but I couldn't understand what they were saying. I didn't think the soldiers could either. The one on the far right kept pushing that button that he had used to translate English earlier. However, he grumbled under his breath as he looked toward the other three. Although I wasn't educated on his alien species, I could tell he was frustrated. I didn't think he had a program in there that could translate what Sally and her friends were saying.

I began to lose focus on the soldiers when the once-purple man suddenly moved his hands while they were behind his back and made his gun disappear. Then his arms quickly shot up above both of our heads, and I saw his hands glowing. I was astonished to find he was holding some sort of bright blue orb, and he threw the light at the four soldiers. I had no idea what it was, so I wasn't sure if I should run, stand still, or brace myself. So, instead, I stepped in front of Sally to try and protect her from whatever was going to happen.

Sally, who had not yet let go of my hand, pulled hard and started us all running again. I couldn't take my gaze from the orb until it created a massive blast of blue light that blinded me. My companions continued to run past the soldiers, who I assumed were blinded like me. I could only guess that Sally and her friends were immune to the light and could still see. Once again, and worse than before, I was tripping over fallen branches and rocks. My arm ached as Sally jerked hard on my hand. I kept waiting to be able to see again, but the blindness lasted the whole time we ran, which was probably about thirty seconds.

When we finally stopped, the bright blue light had vanished, and I could see the singed earth again. I tried to get a good look around me, but then something strange happened. Just seconds after we'd stopped running, Sally forcefully looked at me and ordered, "Don't move or let go of my hand. Try to clear your thoughts."

It was an odd statement. I assumed she was going to tell me something important, but instead, I started to feel a chill at my feet. I didn't think anything of it at first, but then the cold feeling quickly flowed up my legs, tickled my bare hands, and rose to my neck. Before I even had a chance to react, a cool feeling surrounded my face and caused me to gasp.

Sally's hand disappeared from my grasp.

For a second, everything was black. The singed terrain was gone; Sally was gone. All that remained was the cool feeling and the darkness. My breathing became erratic. I rubbed my eyes, trying to incite my vision again. I reached out desperately, hoping to find Sally's hand. But then I began to see. Sally and the pair stood silently staring at me. But when I started to look around, I realized we were no longer in the forest.

My jaw dropped. I couldn't believe what was around me. We were in a small dark green room. Sally reached for my hand, but out of shock, I quickly jumped back and hit a wall; I felt my eyes widen and my jaw open. I almost fell to the floor, but Sally placed her hands on my shoulders. I looked at her with what I was sure was a blank expression. She gave me a small smile and touched my face with her left hand.

"We're leaving now," she said sweetly.

It was amazing how calm she had become. I felt my head slowly shaking back and forth, but she continued to smile with her hand on my face. It was a little bit like the pitiful smile she had given me earlier before the attack. But it was still very kind. And it was much nicer to see her so calm. "Try to stay close to Talents, Sayrah, or me."

"W—who?" I asked, still looking blankly at her.

She let out a little laugh and stepped back from me as she dropped her hand. "The two people who've been running with us," she said. "Their names are Talents and Sayrah."

The woman raised her hand and looked over at me as she began walking out of the room. There was a small curved archway lining the door that I assumed exited the room. "I'm Sayrah," she said in a monotone voice. "And thanks for referring to us as 'the two people running with you.' Real loving MOTHER." She abruptly stopped talking before leaving the room through the archway.

"Sayrah..." Sally called after her, but she had vanished. She looked at the man. "I'm trying to ease Knor into this world."

The man walked over to me and picked up my limp hand to shake it. "I'm Talents," he whispered in a soothing voice. He smiled at Sally and said, "It's ok," then turned away to exit the small room, too.

Sally sighed, took a deep breath, and looked at me. "Come on," Sally said as she moved her hand and motioned for me to follow her.

I did as I was instructed. I couldn't think of anything else to do. Those people knew much more about what was going on than I did.

We walked under the small green archway and entered a new area. I was again frozen with shock. The room was almost one large window, but I wasn't looking at trees or grass or buildings; I was looking at stars. We appeared to be in space, surrounded by darkness.

I glanced at Sally, who still had a smile on her face. I didn't know what to say. Luckily, she did.

"You're in space," she said. "We're in a ship that's nestled on the side of the moon that faces opposite of Earth. We're about to leave and travel to our planet." She turned away for a second, but before I could speak or get a good look at this window room, Sally looked back at me and exclaimed, "Oh, and by the way, my name isn't Sally. It's Tierly."

I gazed at Tierly, startled. I supposed I should have anticipated her name may not be what I thought it was. And someone had said her name during the attack. I just didn't pick up on it till now. However, I just stared at her—stared at the woman who officially wasn't the person I knew anymore.

Maybe I should have run when I had the chance.

Suddenly, as I was staring into the abyss of darkness that was space, everything began to hit me. My heart pounded, and my eyes darted back and forth, looking for something I knew or understood. Dizziness overcame me, and in a split second, I saw nothing but blackness.

Chapter Five

As I walked out of the teleportation room, I'll admit I was relieved. I had been worried for a moment on Earth when Mother couldn't teleport us out. We have the technology to teleport, but there has to be a connection to the ship. The Zyeens had a signal jammer spread all over Earth so no one could leave, but those things are never foolproof. Lots of breaks in the signal. Since we found a break, we were able to teleport onto the ship. Mother does have the ability to teleport us without a signal but she was too weak to protect us with her force field.

We made it to the ship, which was a relief. Now we were all safe. But I glanced to my side and saw this human standing next to me in the teleportation room. It was a room I knew well so seeing an unfamiliar face was upsetting. Or at least annoying. Mother introduced us. I mustered up a wave but walked out of the room in a huff.

However, my emotions took a turn. As I began to relax, I was overcome with dread. My eyes began stinging as the first sign of tears to come. I quickly ran through the dark hallway to my room. I frantically pushed the hand-sized button on the outside of my room and the door slid open. I jumped in and shut it quickly behind me. I fell with my back against the door as tears finally escaped my eyes. "It happened again," I said aloud in disbelief.

I remember many years ago when the Zyeens attacked the planet we were living on. I had finally found someone who was like me. His name was Ogy. He wasn't a Link, but he was a long-living Messan. I was a little young for love and life partners. But what can I say? We were meant to be. I wasn't angry around him like I normally was around others. He made me kind. He brought out the best in me.

But then the Zyeens came. Every time we created a better forcefield or warning system, it took several years, but the Zyeens always advanced and found us.

Everyone rushed to the ships. Ogy stayed behind to help the young and elderly. I waited and waited till it was milliseconds before the first attack. The one that kills most living organisms like the fiery attack on Earth. Mother began to close the door. I screamed and tried to stop her, but Talents had hold of me. I begged her to wait. But I knew we didn't have time.

We were the last ship to leave. We barely made it out. But I lost part of my soul that day.

Now, I sat on the ground against the door, lip quivering and tears falling endlessly.

I sat for a while, but eventually, my grumpy side kicked in. I didn't wanna cry anymore. Ogy was gone and there was nothing I could do, no tears could be spilled, to bring him back. I sniffed a little and gained my composure. "No more crying," I said aloud.

I thought about staying in my room and relaxing, but I wanted to talk to Mother. I wanted to know what we were going to do with our little hitchhiker. I made my way into the control room to wait for her. The vast window showed space as well as a small part of the moon. I will admit, the sight of the universe expanding in front of me never lost its appeal. We had been on Earth for a few years, and I had forgotten the majesty of being so close to the stars.

Talents walked into the room behind me and gave me a funny look.

"What?" I stared at him.

"Be nice," he whispered sternly. I rolled my eyes.

I heard Mother's footsteps, followed by the hitchhiker named Knor. He entered the room, bewildered. His eyes were wide and he hesitated in the entryway. I wanted to go over and push him toward the window just to see his reaction, but I resisted the urge. He didn't it make very far in and I could tell he was starting to panic. His shoulders raised and lowered rapidly, his skin slightly glistened with sweat and his eyes were so wide I thought they would fall out. This was his make-or-break moment: how was he going to handle being in space? But as I suspected, it was too much, and he fell to the floor with a hard thud.

"Be nice?" I asked as I looked at Talents, then at the limp body on the floor. "He's a child! This is the second time he has passed out. It's been 5 minutes."

"No, this is the first time," Talents refuted.

"No, he passed out on Earth," I responded. Talents thought about this for a minute but simply shrugged his shoulders. Mother was crouched next to him on the floor. "I can't believe we are stuck with him."

"Sayrah," Talents said sternly. "Mother loves him so we will love him too."

"Ha!" I walked over to the entryway. "You can love him all you want. I'm going to get a snack. You all can deal with him."

***

I didn't feel like I was asleep for long. It was just enough time for me to have a strange dream about those four soldiers who threatened us on Earth. In my dream, the soldiers were even larger than their real-life eight-foot demeanor. Instead of helmets covering their face, glowing red eyes lit up dark shadowy faces while large fangs jutted out of their mouths. They had placed a tracking meter on me, and just when I thought I was safe, the soldiers appeared on the ship. I tried to escape by running, but I couldn't move my legs. They walked over to me with sly, evil grins stained on their faces. I tried to scream, but one of the soldiers put his hand aggressively over my mouth. Before they had a chance to kill me, I snapped myself awake, heart pounding.

When I quickly sat up, I was in the last place I thought I would be: fully clothed in a tub full of warm—jelly? I wondered how I was breathing while I was asleep and submerged in whatever the stuff was. I cautiously touched the substance with my hand. It felt warm and slimy, but when I retracted my hand, it wasn't wet or sticky. Confused, I touched my hair, and it was dry. I tried to splash the jelly out of the tub, but it wouldn't go over the lip. It stopped right at the top like a wall was blocking it; I could move outside the lip of the tub, but the liquid wouldn't. "Strange," I said aloud.

I looked around the room suspiciously; I was the only one there. The room was covered in a shiny black metal material and it was in the shape of an oval. Fist-sized oval lights covered the ceiling. They were blinding if I stared too long. I didn't see anything in the room that looked like a light switch. I couldn't imagine that those were always on, not if the room was meant for sleeping.

Of course, maybe Sally's—Tierly's—species slept in the light. The thought made the nausea return. I rested my chin on the warm tub but kept my eyes open while I glanced around the room again. There were no windows. For a moment I remembered the vastness of space that I had seen. I shivered a little with fear, but it began to be replaced by temporary excitement. I was in space, on a spaceship. I suddenly wanted to see the stars again.

I couldn't believe I was in space. It made me both excited and frightened. Before I could think about it too much, I heard a knock, but I wasn't sure from where. I lifted my head and looked around the room. The black walls were covered with symbols that I didn't understand. Nothing stood out that looked like a door until part of the wall near my feet at the end of the room lifted up, and Sally—Tierly— stood there.

I closed my eyes. "I don't think I'll ever get used to calling you 'Tierly,'" I said in a soft voice.

"You will," Tierly said gently.

I didn't like it when she spoke to me like that. She acted like she knew what I was going through. But how could she know? I think she could tell I was frustrated because she came over and sat down beside me on the thin edge of the tub. She placed her hand on my shoulder.

"This is going to be hard for you, I know," she said in that same tone.

I shook her hand off. "How do you know?" I asked as I stood up aggressively in the jelly tub and faced her. "Have you done this before? Woken up one morning and thought you were going to receive your second degree but instead watched your planet get destroyed? Planned on marrying someone, only to discover they're really a stranger?!"

Angry, I forgot I was in a tub and tried to walk out. I ended up tripping and falling out onto my face, but at least I was dry. Tierly stood up and tried to help me up, but I quickly got to my feet and shrugged her away. I walked to an area of the room that I had to pretend was the corner. I lost control of my breath. I couldn't speak. I couldn't even look at her. There was so much more I had to say, but maybe it wasn't the time. She'd only been in the room with me for thirty seconds, and I already needed a break from our conversation. I didn't realize until that moment how angry I was at her. It was going to be harder than I thought to talk. I didn't look at her face, but I could feel her gaze lingering on me.

I didn't know what to do, so I stayed standing a few feet away from her. I placed my hands on the wall in front of me. It was as smooth as it looked, but the deep blackness was still surprising. I closed my eyes and lowered my head. Tierly. It was a beautiful name.

Unexpectedly, a tear fell from one of my eyes. My right hand moved from the wall and wiped the small drop from my cheek. I let out a laugh as I wondered to myself whether her name was spelled like "tear." I shook my head again, chuckled a little, and rubbed my hand down my face. There was so much going on, yet how to spell Tierly's name was what my mind chose to focus on. I turned around to look at her.

I was wrong about where her gaze was; she hadn't been looking at me at all. When I turned around, she was looking down. She had a tiny frown on her face, but as I looked at her, she lifted her head and gave me a smile. She appeared somewhat embarrassed. That was when I realized she probably had no idea what to do with me. She must have never expected this to happen.

I decided not to smile back. I wasn't ready to be accommodating. I glanced around the room again as I looked for a window I knew wasn't there. In the room I passed out in, I could see the stars, and Sally had said we were near the moon. I looked back toward her and asked, "Can we see Earth from here?"

Tierly tilted her head to the side a bit and squinted her eyes slightly. I didn't think she expected that question.

She lifted her hand and scratched her eyebrow for a second, then answered, "Well, yes… we can see it from the control room. But I don't think you want to see it right now."

"Well, if I don't see it now," I started, "when will I ever get to see it again? You said we were going somewhere, didn't you?"

It was her turn to take a deep breath and let out a little sigh. "That's true," she said quietly. "This may be the last time you can see it. And we *are* leaving." She stood up and walked over to me slower than I thought she would. Then she reached out her hand for me to take hold of it. "Come with me," she said. "But I warn you, Earth won't look like the Earth you're expecting to see."

With our eyes locked but her smile gone, I took her hand. They were such beautiful, powerful hands. She still wore the oval amethyst I had given her as an engagement ring. She saw me look at the ring, and we both briefly stared at it for a moment. I let go of her hand. It was an awkward moment. Neither of us knew what to say about the ring. I hadn't considered asking her to take it off—it really wasn't my ring, anyway. I'd given it to her to do with as she pleased. Even if I wanted to, I wasn't sure I could ask her to give it back.

Luckily, Tierly broke the silence.

"Follow me," she whispered as she led me out of the room. "I'll take you to the control room." She walked out through the still-open doorway. Before I stepped into the corridor, I poked my head out first. Outside the room was a hallway going both left and right that was made of the same black material as the room I was standing in. Tierly went to the right, and after examining the hallway, I followed her. I reached out my hand to feel the wall. It was just as smooth as the surface in the other room.

It was a small passageway, not much taller than me. I took a sharp curve to the right. I turned my head to see behind us while Tierly continued to move forward. The hallway curved around behind us as well. I could see a bright light behind me glowing around the corner. It was slowly disappearing as we made our way through the curved hallway. My curiosity continued to increase, but I turned back around so I wouldn't run into the wall in front of me.

"What's that bright light?" I asked.

"I'll yell at you about that later," she answered without turning to look at me.

We were only in the black hallway for about ten seconds until we reached what looked like a dead end. But Tierly never stopped. She simply walked through the wall and disappeared. I froze and stood there for a moment pondering what to do next, but before I even decided, Tierly's head popped out through the wall.

"Come on," she said. "Just walk right through."

"Uh… Why doesn't this door have a button to open and close?" I asked.

"That's only for rooms to keep people out," she said. "For privacy. This is just a hallway door," she said as if it all made sense. "Now, come on!"

She disappeared again, and I slowly made my way forward. I reached out my hand to touch the black wall in front of me, but all I felt was warm, moist air, and my hand disappeared. I almost jumped back in disbelief, but before I had a chance to recoil completely, a dark purple hand grabbed tight on my hand and pulled. I catapulted through the wall. As I stumbled, there was a split second of humid darkness, but then there was a dim light, and I ran right into the woman from earlier. Sayrah, I believe her name was, and she was dark purple again.

She dropped my hand and quickly pushed me off her with a scowl on her face. "Don't be such a baby," she growled.

For a moment, I was angry—angry that she was behaving hostilely toward me. I took a deep breath to say something to her, but then I was silenced by the beauty of space. I was once again mesmerized by the clear walls and the tiny stars. I felt engulfed by the universe, surrounded by perfection. Then I remembered Earth and what had happened to it. I wondered whether there was anything left. I glanced over at Tierly. She appeared to be sad, but I didn't know what to do, so I just continued to stand there.

"Do you want to see Earth?" Tierly asked in a monotone voice. Her facial expression never changed. There was little inflection in her question.

"Yes," I answered after a short pause.

She pursed her lips and turned her head to the guy in the room. I think his name was Talents. I had been so taken aback by the stars that I didn't even see him. He looked like he had been staring at us the whole time. His eyes were wide, and he kept staring with a confused look. Maybe I had woken up earlier than he'd expected I would. Or maybe he forgot I was on the ship. He was sitting in a clear glass chair with a large water-like panel in front of him. Those same strange squiggles that were on Tierly's glass tablet, as well as on the walls in the room I woke up in, appeared on that clear water. The water floated in a three-foot-thin rectangular shape.

"Talents," Tierly started, "show him." Talents slowly shook his head, but Tierly persisted. "He needs to see it," she said.

He closed his eyes and turned back around in his chair. He continued to shake his head. His hands slowly moved over the water and floating symbols, and they began to move and change. I couldn't figure it out. His hands weren't wet, and the floating symbols kept transforming. Suddenly, the dark star-filled view through the windows began to shift.

I lost my balance from the quick motion and fell to the ground right on my knees. For a millisecond, a soft pink light flashed brightly. Then there was Earth, right in front of me. But it didn't look like the pictures I had seen in science magazines. It wasn't blue with cloud formations painted over the surface. There weren't beautiful land masses or obvious continents. Instead, the whole planet was on fire. It glowed like a lump of large hot coal. The strange square ships that had attacked the surface were still there, but there weren't as many. I tried to take a deep breath, tried to take in what I was seeing, but I couldn't.

The panic was returning. I felt like I was going to pass out again. Luckily, this time, I was already on the ground.

Tierly came over quickly and fell to her knees in front of me. She placed her hand on my leg. "I'm sorry," she whispered.

But I couldn't take my eyes off my planet as it burned.

"Why?" I asked as I continued to stare. "I just want to know what provokes someone to destroy an entire planet filled with so many innocent people. What had we done? And why… why did you help me?" I asked. I looked at her and placed my hand aggressively on my chest. My voice began to get choked up. "Why not leave me there to die with the rest? What am I supposed to do now?"

"You're supposed to live," Tierly said forcefully. Her hand gripped tighter to my leg as I stopped fighting back tears.

"And you!" I barked. "Who are you? I thought I knew you better than anyone else in the world, but now a stranger stands in front of me. How dare you try to console me! I don't even know who you are! I'm on a ship of strangers. I don't know anyone anymore. They're all dead!"

I held my cheeks firmly and placed my hands over my eyes as tears dripped quickly down my face and through my fingers.

"And who says this isn't some kind of illusion?" I sadly suggested. "Maybe Earth is fine, and you just needed a good excuse to kidnap me." I knew that idea was probably a long shot, but I didn't know what else to say.

I heard someone blurt out a laugh and looked to see it was Sayrah. She was still standing near the passageway with the invisible door. She continued to chuckle as she looked over at Tierly.

"Now, why did we bring him with us again?" Sayrah stood beside the doorway, amused. It felt somewhat rude for her to be laughing as I sat there crying. But she continued to smile. "Oh, yeah," she started. "Because someone," she looked directly at Tierly, "can't keep her hands to herself."

"Sayrah!" Talents shouted from his chair. "Now isn't the time."

"Oh, she looks fine," Sayrah said.

"I'm not worried about Tierly," Talents said.

I realized he was defending me.

"Right," she said as she rolled her eyes. "We have a stowaway. I'll just keep my mouth shut until we get back to Maltina."

"Not now, Sayrah," Tierney said. "Please, just give him some time."

Sayrah glowered at Tierly. She obviously had some feelings she wanted to express but was getting shut down by Talents and Tierly.

"Ugh, fine," Sayrah said as she crossed her arms. "I'll try to be nice."

At that point, I was fed up with the whole situation. Tierly was supposed to be the love of my life, but all she had done was lie. And that Sayrah woman, she seemed to be angry at me although I had done nothing to her. I was tired of all the beating around the bush, so I spoke up.

"You don't have to be nice," I said as I wiped the tears from my face and stood up. Tierly tried to stop me, but I pushed her hand away. "I don't need time. Whatever you need to say to Tierly, you can say with me here."

For a moment, all three of them were taken back. They all looked shocked and confused. Sayrah was the first to come out of the trance. She gave an amused smile and looked over at me. "Huh," she started, "maybe I will like this guy."

"Knor, why don't you and I go talk for a bit?" Tierly said.

"No!" I shouted. "I want to hear what Sayrah has to say."

The smile on Sayrah's face got bigger and more enthused, while Tierly glared at her, seemingly for having started the conversation.

"Well," Sayrah began, "I'm pissed at her because she decided to fall in love while she was only temporarily visiting a planet. Not only is that stupid, but it's also against our rules. I mean, what did she think? Even if your planet hadn't been attacked, which I *am* sorry about, by the way, her life span is way longer than yours. You would have eventually realized she wasn't human anyways. Or something would have had to 'happen,'" she said with air quotes. "She would have had to pretend to leave you or pretend to die or something. Now we have a hitchhiker. I'm not a big fan of hitchhikers."

"What do you mean you are not a fan of hitchhikers?" I asked. Sayrah had bombarded me with all that information, but I could only focus on one thing at a time, especially since everything she said was a direct attack on me.

"Uhhh." She hesitated, staring at me for a minute. I didn't think she expected that question. "Well… I just don't. They can be… a hassle," she answered defensively. She let out a loud breath, stomped her way across the room, and disappeared through another false wall. It seemed like she was done talking.

Sayrah coming in had probably been a blessing in disguise. She'd taken my mind off the destroyed, burning planet on the screens behind me. My breathing returned to normal. I closed my eyes for a moment, standing by Tierly. "Can I go back to my room?" I asked Tierly. I took one last look at the burning planet. "I'm only guessing it's my room. I think I need to rest. Alone."

Those words seemed to sting Tierly, but what else could I say? My planet was gone, and the love of my life had deceived me. And it was a big lie. Not something simple like saying she brushed her teeth when she didn't. She'd lied about something huge. She wasn't even human! I needed some time alone to process everything that was happening.

She nodded her head and walked back over to the entrance of the passageway and disappeared through the wall. I hesitated for a moment then stood up stoically and walked through the wall, the damp air passing around me. We walked down the dark hallway together, her a few feet in front of me. She stopped outside an open door and used her arm to motion me inside. I walked past her and stood right beyond the doorway.

I said, "Thank you for leading me to the room. I probably would have gotten lost looking for this place."

She lightly placed her hand on a small square-shaped symbol near the door I hadn't noticed before. "If you press it once," she began, "the door will close. If you press it twice, it will open." Then she reached into her pocket and pulled out a strange oval-shaped black device. It was about the size of a small car alarm remote. She reached out her hand to give it to me. "If you give this a good little tap, it'll connect to me like a cell phone. You can call me if you need me. It's called a pendant."

I looked at the oval-shaped object suspiciously. It didn't look like a cell phone or any kind of electronic for that matter. It just looked and felt like a smooth rock. But I said, "Okay," and put it in my shirt pocket.

Tierly lingered outside the threshold of the door. She seemed to have something to say, but I didn't want to hear it. I had so many questions, but I couldn't bear to ask them yet. So I pressed the button once and let the door close in her face.

Chapter Six

After I had eaten a small snack of orange grains with pickled fruit, I spent a little time by myself in my dark room. I lay on my bed and threw a black and white checkered hacky sack up and down, switching hands as I caught it before it hit my face. It was the only thing I had taken to the ship a couple of years ago, so, other than my clothes, it was the only memento I had from my time on Earth.

I wanted to talk to Mother. I wanted to know why she wanted to be with this human so much. I wanted to know why she broke one of our rules.

We had a few rules we followed when we visited other planets. Stuff like don't show anyone your powers and stay cloaked at all times, even in our home. I'll admit, Talents and I were known to break the cloaking rule when we were in our home. But that didn't seem like a big deal. However, Mother breaks a very important rule that affects more than just her: she falls in love. I have never considered dating a species that lives such a short lifetime. It doesn't seem fair to anyone. I wanted to scold her for being stupid.

I sat up determined and made my way to the control room, leaving my hacky sack behind. Talents was sitting at the helm with Mother sitting beside him. She heard me come in, turned, and smiled.

"I was about to come get you," Mother said. I scowled. I was so angry and I think I figured out why, but I didn't want to admit it to anyone, even myself. But I couldn't deny that I was angry because I was jealous. I love Mother more than anyone or anything in the whole universe. Just looking at her now after she had been away from us for a couple of years I almost melted with happiness to see her (even if I was also pissed at her). But seeing the way she felt for that human made me feel like I was losing her. And losing my mother would probably kill me, which is why what she said next hurt so much. "I need to talk to you two."

I walked over to the large window at the pink light of energy that shined through while we were traveling. It wouldn't be too much longer and we would be at Maltina, our home planet. Mother stood up from her clear chair that vanished like melting ice as soon as she stood. She walked over to me and put her hand on my shoulder. I turned and smiled at her. She was the only one I would smile for. And even though I was hurt, I still loved her deeply.

"Something happened," Mother started as she moved her hand to guide me to turn around. "It happened the first few days we came to Earth. I…" she trailed off and looked down, sighing as she removed her arm from me and rubbed her forehead.

"Is everything okay?" I asked, concerned for Mother, dread suddenly overwhelming me. Talents stood up from his seat and came over to us. He was also concerned.

We stood together for a moment while Mother composed herself. A couple of liquid metal tears fell from her eyes, and she wiped them away before they hardened. Talents and I both placed a hand on either shoulder and looked at her with confusion.

"I'm dying," Mother whispered as she lifted her head and looked back and forth at Talents and me.

"You're what?" I questioned as my voice rose in volume. I shook my head. I had to have heard her incorrectly.

"My love, I'm dying," she said with a somber look in her eyes.

"How do you know?" I asked aggressively, losing my composure.

"My heart. It stopped during the first week on Earth."

"And you didn't tell us till now!?" But before she could answer my question, we heard a loud thump at the entranceway.

***

After talking with Tierly, they closed in her face. And almost before it shut all the way, emotions cascaded over me. My eyes flooded with tears. I fell back against the door and slid down till I sat silently on the floor for a moment as my breath caught up with my emotions. I let out an agonizing sound that filled the room. My whole body convulsed as I continued to relentlessly sob. I thought of my family and friends, tears flowing down my face. I thought of all the things I wanted to tell them, like how much I loved them. But as I cried, all I could hope for was that they didn't suffer, that they weren't scared when it happened. I fell to my side and curled into a fetal position as I moaned and struggled to breathe in between sobs. I didn't care if anyone could hear me.

The ground was surprisingly warm, but I still longed for the comfort of a pillow and blanket.

After what felt like hours, the tears slowly began to dwindle, and my breath became more regulated. I closed my eyes for just a second and immediately slipped into unconsciousness. Suddenly, I was drifting through the clouds on Earth, flying high above snowcapped mountains and beautiful blue-green oceans. I decided to go to my parents' house.

I thought of my father outside playing with our dog Schatzi. He always acted like he hated her but if you couldn't find my father, he was probably outside playing with the dog. My mother would be reading on the porch. She loved reading nutritional books and planning new snacks and meals for the family. My only sibling was my youngest brother. He was twenty and still lived at home. He hadn't quite decided what he wanted to do with his life, but my family was patient. They still didn't think acting was the smartest choice, but they still loved me. However, the peaceful flying quickly turned to horror.

Those metal square ships filled the sky while I was flying around. The cold wind rushed by as I dodged the objects in the atmosphere around me. My skin burned from the icy wind. Then, I saw my house. I changed directions and flew as fast as I could to the ground. I was almost at their house, and I could see them standing outside waving at me. They were calling my name, saying, "Know! Please save us!" I was almost to them when everything abruptly caught on fire. I watched in horror as they screamed, flames surrounding them and everything below me. The burning from the fire heated my whole body. I tried so hard to get to them, but I could no longer move. I floated above them as I watched my mother and father and my brother burn, screaming for me to save them.

I woke up in a panic. Cold sweat dripped from my forehead. My breathing was erratic. I sat up quickly from my fetal position on the warm ground. A few tears escaped my eyes as I tried to relax, focusing on the room around me. The memories of what was currently happening came crashing back into my mind. But I closed my eyes for a moment, taking a few deep breaths. I needed to relax. I couldn't let the overwhelming emotions overcome me again. I whispered to myself, "You're okay. You're safe." My breathing began to slow to normal; my body began to calm down. I decided I needed to do something. I had cried for who knew how long, and then I had slept for a while. I wondered what time it was. How long had I been asleep? I stupidly pulled my phone out of my pocket. A blank screen showed up. There was nothing left it was connected to. I decided I should find out how long I had been on this ship. I was rested, so I assumed I'd slept for multiple hours. Also, I was starving.

I could either do something productive or sit there and wallow in self-pity. It was time to get my shit together.

I wondered what I should do next. I could stay in the room and—well, I guess just sit. I could also explore the ship, although that didn't seem like a good idea. Considering I couldn't open or even find the door when I first got there, who knew what other surprises the ship held? I might want to wait until someone could lead me around and show me everything. But while I was thinking about what to do, I already knew the answer; the best idea seemed to be to talk to Tierly or at least go find her. The only place I knew how to get to was the control room. I hoped she would be in there.

I stood up from my position on the floor and looked at the door. I hesitated but then pushed the button once and waited for it to open. Nothing. Crap. Then I remembered: once to close, two times to open. I reached over and pushed it twice. I hoped it no longer registered that first push—I had no idea what would happen if I pushed it three times.

Thankfully, the door opened, and I cautiously made my way through. I headed to the right, down the hallway, and toward the control room. The fake doorway was still there, but I noticed a soft pink color seeping from the edges. I wondered what it was, but I got distracted by voices. I could also hear Tierly talking to someone. I couldn't understand them, but it wasn't the same language I had heard before. That one was soft and breathy. However, it wasn't a calm conversation. Sayrah's words were sharp, and she spoke quickly. Talents chimed in with the same sharp tone before grunting and yelling.

I quickened my pace, but I paused right at the doorway to the control room door. I no longer saw the darkness of space through the large window. Instead, only a pink light shone. I wondered why the window had a pink glow and I couldn't see the vastness of space. However, at least for a moment, I was more focused on the… beings in the room. Tierly, Talents, and Sayrah all stood in a triangle in the middle of the room. Tierly had her back to me, but I could see Talents' and Sayrah's faces. They looked like they'd just gotten the worst news they had ever heard. Sayrah had her hand over her mouth as tears trickled down her face. Talents just looked shocked, presumably unable to speak or move. I realized I had interrupted something big, but it wasn't like they just lost all their family and friends as I had. The thought caused me to almost spiral and cry, but I took a deep breath and closed my eyes.

I told myself to stay calm. I opened my eyes, let out a sigh, and noticed everyone had changed clothes. All three of them wore what looked like cotton nightgowns that were a pale green. Even Talents had on a gown, which looked a little weird on his muscular frame. But then again, I was learning something new every second. I wasn't completely sure of anyone's gender or what was considered proper dress for their—species. Another weird thing was Talents and Sayrah were also dark purple again.

I took a step to go through the doorway but suddenly slammed face-first into a clear wall. I fell back and grabbed my nose. Luckily it wasn't bleeding but it definitely hurt. After my embarrassment and confusion, Tierly turned to look at me. Sayrah and Talents were still staring at Tierly. She came over and pushed the side of the wall and the clear glass vanished.

I said, "I'm sorry. Should I leave?"

'We wanted to give you some privacy," Tierly said calmly. "You sounded… upset."

I blushed a little. They heard me having a fucking meltdown. I was mildly embarrassed, but remembered I had been through a lot so I felt justified in my reaction.

Sayrah and Talents finally noticed me. Sayrah removed her hand from her shocked face and looked back at Tierly as tears continued to fall down her face. Sayrah shook her head and pushed Tierly out of the way as she made her way quickly down the passageway on the other side of the control room. It was open, but she pushed a button as she disappeared, and suddenly I could see a faint glass door (like the one before that I hadn't seen because of the bright light).

Talents let out a small laugh and sat back down in his clear chair. He whispered something I didn't understand, but I assumed it was a different language. But he switched and began speaking in English, I assume for me. "You should have fucking told us," he said in a disappointed tone. "Don't go anywhere, Knor. We're done talking."

"Talents," Tierly protested as she turned to look at Talents. "Just listen—"

"No!" Talents yelled. "We're done for now. Go try and explain everything to Knor. I'm sure he is confused." Talents turned away from her and sat back in the glass chair. He began interacting with the water table again. He just kept shaking his head and letting out small laughs.

I noticed something strange on his wrist; it was the same thick bracelet cuff that Tierly always wore, except he was golden. Did Sayrah have one as well? I wanted to ask him about it, but I wasn't sure how important that question was. I had thousands of things I wanted to ask, and jewelry just didn't seem like a priority.

Tierly took a deep breath and turned back toward me. From across the room, she stared into my soul with a sad smile. "I'll be back in a moment," Tierly whispered and disappeared after Sayrah. I was curious as to what she had told them, but I could tell that also wasn't a question to ask right then.

"Should I be concerned?" I asked Talents.

"Well…." he started, "it's not great. I'll let her tell you."

"Knor, how old are you?" Talents asked.

"I'm 27," I answered.

"So you are old enough to know women are crazy?" Talents said with a wink. I let out a small laugh. We stood in silence for a few moments.

"Can I…" I began, "Touch the pink light?" I paced over to the window and was about to reach my hand out when Tierly appeared. She looked a little stressed but gave me a small smile. I decided to do my best and ask her some questions. I asked the most basic question I could think of to loosen the slight tension in the room that I noticed when I saw Talents scowling at Tierly. "So," I started, "what happened to space? I thought it was black, not pink."

Tierly perked up. The somber smile on her face changed. She beamed brightly and looked excited. She walked over quickly, lifted her hands, and opened her mouth. Then she clasped her hands together and stared at me for a moment before closing her mouth and letting out a soft laugh. She raised one hand to run her fingers through her short sand-colored hair. She was obviously nervous. "Uh…," she began, "It's kind of complicated. Has to do with quantum mechanics and traveling fast. So….I.. well, uh… hmmm?"

I smiled a little. "Don't know where to start?" I asked. Tierly shook her head. It was cute to see her flustered. "How about you show me the ship? That way, I won't get lost without you."

"Honestly, it isn't very big," Tierly answered as she looked around the room. "It's just one large circle. Can't really get lost. You may forget which door leads to your room, but if you just keep walking, you'll simply end up back at the control room." Tierly suddenly got really enthusiastic again and grabbed my hand. "Come with me! I'll show you the heart of the ship." She pulled my hand, but I didn't budge.

She stopped to see what the problem was and she saw me gazing at our hands. I wasn't sure what to say, but at that moment, I didn't feel like we should be holding hands. It just didn't feel right. We weren't a couple anymore. At least, we weren't in my mind. After realizing she was a stranger whom I knew nothing about, I couldn't imagine still being in a relationship with her.

Tierly frowned and slowly dropped my hand. "Sorry," she whispered as she turned away from me. "Come on," she said, turning back with a smile as she tried to rekindle the positivity she'd originally had. "Follow me."

I accompanied her through the control room past Talents as he sat at the control panel. He turned his head and eyed me as we walked past. I thought, for a second, that he was glaring at me, but then he gave me a slight wink and smile and returned to his task. Tierly and I made our way to the second passageway that connected to the control room. I had yet to be down that way, but I had seen Sayrah come and go through there. I wondered where she was and if she was okay. She and Talents were clearly mad at Tierly for something, but I still didn't want to ask.

Tierly spoke up as we were walking down the passageway. "The three rooms on the right are Talents, Sayrah's, and mine," she said. "The last door on the left is the kitchen."

Although I was listening to what she said, my curiosity was piqued when I saw a bright white light at the end of the hallway. I remembered that at the other end of the passageway where my room was, there was another bright light I had wondered about. That light looked to be the same.

As we made our way down the hallway toward the beam, I noticed I couldn't see past it. It was very bright, but I couldn't see through it. It was a soft color, like a cloud, but completely opaque. Tierly stopped for a moment as we approached the light. I reached my hand out to see if it was actually solid, but my hand simply disappeared. I brought my hand back and looked toward Tierly. She had a surprised look on her face.

"You're very brave to touch the light," she said initially but then laughed. "Maybe a little stupid as well. I wouldn't make it a habit of touching things you don't understand. It's a good way to lose your hand."

I felt my skin flush with embarrassed red heat and looked down at my hands. I felt stupid. My hand was perfectly fine, but she was right. It could have easily been something formidable.

Tierly awkwardly cleared her throat as we stood at the threshold of the light. My curiosity turned into a bit of fear. I wondered what she meant by the "heart of the ship" and what was behind the glowing doorway. Tierly glanced at me and said, "Are you ready?"

I slowly nodded my head, and she motioned for me to follow her as she disappeared into the light.

I hesitated for a second and then finally stood up as straight as I could and whispered to myself, "Don't be a baby. You got this." Then I made my way into the light.

I walked blindly for a few moments and looked all around me. I was surrounded by a fog-like glow. I could look and see my hands in front of me, but I couldn't tell if I could see anything in the room. All I saw was light. I began to panic. I said, "Tierly" in a much sharper tone than I meant to. But I was getting scared. I had walked in a straight line, but what would happen if I couldn't make it out of the room? I turned around and couldn't see the exit. I reached my hands out, fearing I might walk into something. But then within the light, Tierly appeared. My panic subsided; I wouldn't be trapped in there forever. But I did decide to stay very close to her for the rest of the time.

Tierly smiled at me and asked, "Would you like to see the heart of the ship?"

I once again nodded slowly, completely unsure of what to expect. Tierly then reached her hands out, and the same type of water-like panel from the control room appeared under her hands. She shifted them back and forth methodically over the sparkling water. It moved beautifully with her touch. It was as if she were a painter; it was mesmerizing. But then, for a split second, the room went completely dark, and the terror I'd recently felt returned.

However, it didn't last long. The control panel had a slight glimmer, so I could see Tierly's hands. She pushed them both deep into the water and when she lifted them up, the room began to spin. There were no longer any walls; the whole room, including the floor, turned into space and what looked like intricate galaxies spread out all around me. I could see them spinning!

I lifted my hand to touch them, but I paused. Tierly had told me not to just touch everything I see, so I asked, "What happens if I reach my hand out?"

"I wouldn't do that if I were you," she said. "You can walk around the room, but don't touch the galaxies. If you do, you'll destroy them."

"Destroy them?" I said, confused.

"Yes," she answered. "This may be hard to believe, but those are real galaxies. If you touch them, you'll obliterate them."

"What do you mean they're real galaxies?" I asked, still confused. "How can you fit a galaxy into a small room?"

"Unfortunately, it would take me your entire lifetime to explain this process," she answered. "And even then, you probably wouldn't understand. But these are actual galaxies that we've collected. Touching them will terminate them."

I stood still for a moment and tried to process what she was saying. Intrigued, I asked, "Do… people live in these galaxies?" I stepped back from one that was spinning a few feet in front of me.

"No," Tierly answered. "None of these galaxies have the proper planet placement to form life."

"So…" I started, "why do you collect galaxies then?"

"Oh, they power the ship, Knor," she said quickly. "Each of these galaxies has a black hole at the center of it. As the matter within the galaxies is destroyed, it produces energy. We use that energy to run the ship."

"So, these are real galaxies?"

"Yes."

"And if I touch them, they'll be destroyed."

"Yes."

"Man," I said after a long pause. "This is trippy. Your ship is powered by black holes, and these are all real galaxies somehow being stored on a small ship. Wow. I knew I was probably going to see a lot of strange, unexplainable stuff, but this really is incredible." I laughed as I cautiously looked around the room. I kept my distance, but I wondered how cool it would be to tell someone I destroyed a galaxy. Of course, I had no one to tell.

Suddenly, a wave of sadness flowed over me; I remembered my family and friends were all gone. And as amazing as the moment was, I couldn't help but let a few tears stream down my face. I smiled a sad smile as I thought of my family.

But my sadness quickly turned to anger. It hit me unexpectedly, and I spoke out more sharply than I expected. "How could you say that you don't have room on this ship?!" I shouted.

Tierly stood in silence; a shocked look stained her face. "What do you mean?" she asked calmly but also looking confused.

"You told me on Earth before we left that there wasn't enough room for anyone else," I said sharply with a stream of tears flowing down my cheeks, my heart racing. "But look at this place! We could have easily saved more people." I turned away from Tierly as I wiped my tears. I took a few deep breaths. I was worried I would pass out again.

After a few breaths, my heart rate started to fall back to a normal pace, and the tears stopped falling. I turned around and looked back at Tierly. She stood in silence with her head down. I wasn't sure what she was thinking. I looked around the room again as the amazement of the trapped galaxies flowed through me.

Tierly lifted her head and spoke. "We didn't have time, Knor. We couldn't save your family. If they had been at the graduation, then maybe. But I couldn't have teleported us to them. I used all my strength to protect us from the first wave. I'm sorry. I wish… I wish I could have saved them."

She lifted her hand over the flowing control panel again and snapped her fingers. All of a sudden, the galaxies and darkness vanished, and the room returned to the soft light. Tierly closed her hand into a fist, and the water-like panel disappeared. She motioned for me to follow her, and remembering the panic I had about being trapped in the room, I followed quickly behind, almost stepping on her heels.

We exited on the opposite side of where we came in, so we were in the hallway that led to my room. Tierly motioned for me to enter the other doorway to my left. I stood for a moment, thinking. I saw the symbol on the door that was meant for opening and closing. Twice to open or twice to close? For the life of me, I couldn't remember.

Tierly laughed and reached around me. "It's twice to open," she said with a smile as she pushed the button. The door slid open.

But before I walked in, I peeked my head through the doorway to see inside. I was taken aback by the room. The rest of the ship I had seen so far was completely black. That room, however, was all white, and the only thing inside was a small cot on the right side. It looked like an army cot, taut gray cloth raised about two feet off the floor. Just big enough for a person to lay down on.

Tierly slipped around me, entering the room, keeping as much distance between us as she could in the small doorway. She walked over to the piercing white wall on the left side of the room, put her hand on a small symbol on the wall, and a drawer popped out. I stepped into the room cautiously and walked over to the cot. I was suddenly sleepy, and that was the first real bed I'd seen. I still wasn't sure at all how to use the jelly-filled tub in my room, so the cot seemed a lot more comforting.

Unfortunately, the comforting feeling didn't last long as I watched Tierly pull two long syringes out of the drawer.

Chapter Seven

Mother came to my room shortly after I arrived. Gave me just enough time to get comfortable on my bed. She didn't knock on my door, she just came in, which I expected. I probably wouldn't have let her in if she had knocked. I heard her coming and could have locked the door, but I decided against it. If anything I was conflicted. It was terribly mad, but also I loved her. I didn't want her to be sad because of me ignoring her when we didn't know how much time she had left. Links could live awhile after their hearts had stopped, but it was still a death sentence.

So begrudgingly, I didn't lock the door and let her come on in. But I had a scowl and ended up not being able to control my anger.

Mother walked over to me as I lay on my sleeping bed. Knor had woken in a hibernation bed which was used for healing or extra rejuvenation. But I didn't need that so I was just laying on my small, sand-colored bed. I was throwing my hacky sack still to calm my nerves. It was a repetitive, relaxing motion for me. On Earth, something like that would be stimming. People with autism often did it. After my time on Earth, I did see some similarities to me and people with that characterization. I had been born a little differently than all other Links. Mother always played it off, but she knew I was different. I didn't have quite the same utopia, love-everyone mentality that Links had. Everyone in Maltina loved me anyway, but I only mildly cared for any of them. I mostly cared for Mother and Talents; mostly Mother.

"Got some more important news for me that you should have shared sooner?" I asked, not looking at her. "You know what? Don't bother. I honestly may never speak to you again."

"Sayrah, listen," Tierly pleaded.

"No!" I shouted. "You've betrayed me and Talents. Talents may be more forgiving than I am, but I can't believe what you did to us. You would rather spend the last few years of your life with a stranger than your own family?" I paused while I wiped a few metal tears from my flushed purple cheeks.

We both looked at each other for a moment. I wiped my cheeks a few times to get rid of the metal tears. Mother just stood there staring at me. I wondered to myself how long I would be mad at her. But then I realized I didn't want to be mad forever.

I sighed and looked at her with a stern look. I still didn't want to talk to her.

"Soon I'm going to give Knor the translator nanos." She sat down near my head and caught my toy as it was falling back into my hand.

I sighed. "And what exactly does that have to do with me?"

"Well he is afraid of needles," she said shyly, as if she didn't really want to tell me his secret.

I shot up from my recumbent position. "Really?" I laughed. "Can I be a fly on the wall?"

"You can be in the room, but I need you to be invisible. And never tell him that I let you watch. I just know you are sick and like to watch people squirm." She said this with a wink.

My heart raced. "Now?" I asked excitedly.

Mother sighed, but she gave me an enduring smile. "Go hide in the med bay. I will get Knor and we will meet in the med bay in a few minutes."

While she was talking I had already stood up and made my way to the door. It was time to watch this human hitchhiker squirm.

***

I took a step back, tripping over my feet and falling onto the floor. "What are those?" I asked in a demanding tone. My skin burned with heat and fear. My heart pounded, and I was desperately trying to stand from my place on the floor, but I was so scared I couldn't. It may have been irrational, but my fear of needles was intense.

"These are translator nanos," she said as she held one in each hand. "One is injected into your ears, and one is injected into your eyes. They'll allow you to read and hear different languages."

"Inject!" I shouted desperately at her. "In my eyes?"

"Knor," she started, "Listen to me. It'll be really quick. I know you're terrified of needles, but you have to do this." She took one large step toward me.

I jumped up from the floor. But in my panic, I tripped over my feet again and fell back to the ground. I felt like I was in a cheesy horror movie where the audience was constantly shouting at the screen, "Just get up and run!" But I couldn't seem to stay on my feet.

I looked up at the still-open door and stood again, making my way frantically toward it. She quickly blocked my exit. "Knor," she said again. "Please calm down. It'll just take a second."

"No way!" I said as I shook my head adamantly. I stood only about four feet from Tierly and the door. "You know I can't do needles. And you expected me to let you put them in my eyes and ears? No! No way! After all I've been through, now you want to put a needle in my eye?"

"Knor, look, you'll barely feel it," she said in a stern tone.

Tierly had never been patient with my needle phobia. She didn't understand why I was so frightened. To be honest, I didn't know either. It was an uncontrollable fear. Needles just made me panic.

"Are you really going to make me call Talents in here to hold you down?" she asked with no sympathy at all, just frustration.

"No one is holding me down," I stated firmly. "You can't make me. I'm going to have to be without a translator-whatever."

"Look, my planet is very diverse. There are many different languages spoken, and they don't know English. You won't be able to understand any of them. You must do this. Almost every advanced species has some sort of translation device. It'll be so much easier for you once you have these in. You'll be able to understand everyone."

"Nope," I said defiantly as I looked around her, planning my escape.

Tierly sighed. "Okay. We'll do this the hard way." She placed both syringes in one hand and opened her free hand. One of those strange black rocks that she had given me appeared in her palm, and she pressed down on it.

"Time for translator nanos?" I heard Talents ask through the rock.

"I need your help in the med bay," Tierly stated.

Before I could even blink, Talents was walking through the door. I tensed up; I was ready to fight him. He was a small guy. I was sure I could keep him off me. But suddenly, Talents raised his hand, and I couldn't move. I felt like I was frozen. I tried to run or lift my hands up to protect myself, but nothing happened.

"Thank you," Tierly said as she walked over to my motionless body. As she reached me, she looked at me with a satisfied expression. My eyes were stuck open, and I could barely breathe.

The prick in my first eye felt like fire, and everything glazed over as if I had Vaseline on my eye. She injected the other side, and the same burn and vision change occurred. I couldn't blink; all I could feel were tears streaming down my face. I thought maybe she had messed up since I couldn't see that well at all.

Then she moved on to my ears. The needle went in, and immediately, there was a deep hum in my ear, then she went on to the next. All I could see were Vaseline-covered images, and all I could hear was a deep hum.

Immediately after she was done, Talents lowered his arm, and my breathing returned to normal. I blinked and pushed Tierly away from me.

"Fuck you!" I growled. I went back and forth between rubbing my eyes and rubbing my ears; they stung. I could still feel the prick of the needles. For a moment, the deep buzz in my ears turned into a high-pitched whistle, but there was also thumping. It felt like my ears had a heartbeat. I continued to blink and rub my stinging eyes.

However, after only a few moments, I blinked, and I could see. But everything was different. The ship had changed. The walls were still white and covered with symbols, but I could read them. The writing I had never seen before suddenly made sense to me. I scanned the room, eyes still slightly burning, ears still ringing, but the discomfort was fading.

"Can you see now?" Tierly asked empathetically.

I mustered up a little glare because I was still mad at her, but I was also in shock because she was no longer speaking English.

"Woah," I said. The language was soft and breathy, but I knew what she was saying. It was a very strange feeling. I heard the language as she was saying it, but my mind translated just as fast. It was slightly disorienting to hear one thing and think another.

"It'll be weird at first," she said in her language. "But you'll get used to it."

I continued to stare in awe at all the symbols on the walls I finally understood. When I looked at the door, I knew the one to open and close it said Door Controls and the drawer Tierly had gotten the syringes from said Translator Nanos. I wondered about all the symbols in my room and what they might say.

"Come on," Tierly said, motioning me to exit the room. "I bet you're hungry."

It was a strange thing to realize after everything I had been through, but I was hungry. Starving, honestly. I wasn't sure how long I'd been on the ship. I didn't have a watch or a cell phone anymore, so I couldn't keep track of the time. But it didn't really matter what time it was—I was just hungry.

I made my way past Tierly through the doorway, making sure to give her a small scowl as I walked by. I was still pissed about the needles, even if it was probably a necessary evil.

I stepped into the narrow hallway, paused for a moment, and asked, "The kitchen is on the other side of the ship, correct?"

"Yes," she said as she walked past me.

I looked suspiciously down the passageway. The soft pink light glowed to my left in the control room, and the gentle white light in the heart of the ship gleamed to my right. My room still had the door open. Instead of walking all the way down the passageway to the control room to get to the kitchen, Tierly turned to the right and disappeared through the wall.

I rolled my eyes. Not that again. I didn't like the fake walls. Also, there was no symbol or marker to indicate where the false wall was, so I just had to know or guess. "One of these days," I said to myself, frustrated, "I'm just going to run into a freakin' wall and break my nose." I walked over to the wall, held up my hand out of reflex, and walked through. I felt the warmth and moisture again, but the sensation was over quickly. Within seconds, I was on the other side of the ship.

Tierly stood about six feet away from me to my right in front of an open room. I went over to her and slowly looked in. The room didn't have that many symbols written on the wall. The only thing I saw was something that looked like a small red microwave nestled into the wall with a symbol that read Synthesizer. There were two other symbols I noticed: one read Trash and the other read Table.

I looked at Tierly, still not smiling. "So," I asked, "now what?"

Tierly laughed. "Well, it's real simple," she said. "Put your hand over the synthesizer. Think about what you want to eat. It will beep, then it will open, and then you'll have food."

I looked at her skeptically, raising one eyebrow. I didn't know why I didn't believe her. She hadn't lied to me—at least not since I'd been on the ship. So I decided to try it out. I went over to the synthesizer and put my hand over the symbol. I thought about what I wanted. I imagined anything from blueberry pie to steak but finally focused on some salmon. It beeped, I took my hand off, and it opened. What I'd hoped for was some delicious salmon to appear. However, instead, to my disappointment, it was what looked like an uncooked square of ramen noodles.

Tierly laughed. I, however, frowned, unamused. She had gotten my hopes up for something delicious, and instead, I got ramen. She walked over toward me and grabbed the noodles. "Remember crack noodles?" Tierly asked.

For a moment, I was filled with nostalgia. There was a special brand of noodles that Tierly and I used to make all the time. They were simply a book of noodles with a premade powdered sauce, but we would make them special by adding extra cream, a yummy vegetable, or our own unique seasoning. Anytime one of us had a bad day, we would always make crack noodles to cheer the other one up. They were special because we always spent time together cooking them. They were also so addictive, which is why we said they were crack.

I smiled at her, and she returned it. Briefly, I remembered my love for her and forgot about the lies. I remembered the many nights sitting at the kitchen table drinking wine and eating the delicious crack noodles, talking about the future.

The nostalgia ended while we stood in awkward silence, and I was forced to process my roller coaster of emotions. But eventually, I reached out and grabbed the noodles from her. I was curious if they tasted like ramen noodles. There was no seasoning packet, and there wasn't anything in the room to cook them with. I looked at Tierly, and she nodded at me. So I took a small bite just to appease her, thinking about how quickly I would get tired of eating ramen for every meal.

But something strange happened. It didn't taste like ramen, and as the noodles hit my mouth, they changed texture. They tasted and felt just like a freshly cooked salmon filet marinated in my favorite teriyaki and ginger sauce. I took another bite, shocked at how delicious it was. I looked at Tierly, mouth full of salmon flavor and texture. She laughed at me and said, "See? That's why I told you we call them crack noodles. You thought they were delicious back on Earth. They're even better here because they taste like what you are craving."

Tierly put her hand on the synthesizer, it beeped and opened, and she reached in to grab her dry noodle square that looked just like mine. She took a small bite and let out a sigh. She must have been hungry too. I wondered what hers tasted like. I thought about asking, but a more important question had been weighing on my mind. "Sally—" I started. "Sorry, I mean Tierly." I paused for a moment as a small wave of sadness came over me. I took a deep breath and pushed the feeling down. "Where exactly are we going?"

Tierly walked over to the other side of the small room and I saw a button that had the symbol for Table. She pushed it and walked a few feet away. Out of thin air, a ball of light began to appear where she had been standing. Slowly, it went from a circle of light and shape-shifted. Once the light disappeared, two glass chairs and a small glass table stood on the side of the room.

Tierly motioned with her arm for me to sit. I was slightly hesitant because I had never sat on a glass chair before. But I walked over with my noodles and cautiously sat down. She did the same thing. "So," Tierly said after she swallowed a bite of her noodles, "we're going to a planet called Maltina. But it's not that far away. You actually know this planet. It's in your solar system. You called it Venus."

"What?!" I almost spit out my crack noodles. "We can't be going to Venus. It's uninhabitable. It's too close to the sun. Also, wouldn't humans have known if any of the planets in our solar system had life?"

"It's true that Venus is too close to the sun to produce life," she admitted. "My species didn't originate on Venus, or Maltina, as we call it, but we moved there because… Well, we just needed to. There's a force field over the planet that allows just enough sun to support life. The force field also creates an atmosphere as well as a false atmosphere over the top of it. This false atmosphere is what you know and see. Also, a natural day on Venus is five thousand hours, so we have a mechanism on the planet that causes it to rotate much faster and create proper gravity. So don't worry. It'll be a lot like Earth."

"Oh…" I said, not really understanding. I had a political science degree, but it definitely wasn't that type of science major. All I knew about planets was what I read once in some science magazine while waiting in a doctor's office. It explained why Earth was the only habitable planet in our solar system.

"So how long will it take to get there?" I asked as I took another bite of my noodles.

"Less than an hour," she answered.

I pondered that for a few minutes, slowly eating my crack noodles. I had to admit, I was terrified. I had so many questions and concerns that I didn't know where to start.

Tierly looked at me and answered a question I had only briefly thought to ask. "I'm sure you've noticed that Talents and Sayrah have purple-colored skin. So I need to show you something." I froze, no longer able to eat. Tierly lifted her arm and showed me her silver cuff bracelet that she always wore. She unclipped it, and when she did, she became even more beautiful than she already was. Her hair stayed the same sandy blonde color, but her skin started to glow a lavender tint. The most shocking of all was her eyes. They had always been hazel, but at that moment, they sparkled like emeralds. They glowed like her skin.

I wasn't really sure what to say. I wanted to make a joke about how beautiful our babies would be, but then it hit me that she and I weren't really a couple anymore. So that may have been awkward. But I had to tell her something. I settled on, "Your beauty has me at a loss for words."

Tierly smiled that innocent smile she used to get when I kissed her. It was like she was always surprised when we kissed. It was cute. But the smile and happiness disappeared when I asked my next question.

"Hey," I started, "what were you talking about when I came into the control room earlier? Talents and Sayrah seemed really upset."

Tierly's smile disappeared, and she looked down. She took a deep breath and looked back at me.

"Knor," she said, "I hate to tell you this, but I'm dying."

Chapter Eight

A little over five years ago I was sitting on Maltina taking in our artificially created sunlight on the beach of our artificially created lake. The kids played as they always did by the water. Mother and Talents snuck up on me and scared me on the beach. Links had incredible hearing, but they could also be silent and sneaky. I jumped and scolded them. I was trying to relax.

"I brought Talents to tell you something," Mother said suspiciously.

I sighed, but was curious so I turned around to look at them, although I stayed seated. "What then?" I asked. "What have you come to tell me?"

"We are going to take a trip to Earth," Talents said with a grin. "But Mother won't tell me why all of a sudden she wants to go. We haven't been in a hundred Earth years."

"Exactly! I have been looking at images and listening to their broadcasts. Their technology has greatly advanced. It would be fun to explore, especially since they look almost like us. We will only have to hide our color."

"Tell her the condition," Talents said with a condescending grin.

"Well," Mother started, "I would like to explore by myself. Maybe do some schooling. Learn about history. Stuff like that."

This didn't make me happy. Why does she always want to leave us behind while she explores? So I asked, "Why can't we all stay together?" I love Talents, but normally when we visited a planet, I was stuck with him for a few years.

"I just need some time alone," she said, but she looked at the ground when she did. I felt like there was another reason, but I decided not to care.

"Fine," I said as I turned around back to my relaxing post. "When do we leave?"

***

As I sat with Tierly, for a moment, I thought of our past and my love for her.

I remember as I waited for my first acting class to start, I was filled with nerves. What if acting classes were a waste too? What if I spent all that time and money and still didn't find my purpose? But I held back my fear as best I could and sat anxiously waiting for the auditorium door to unlock. And that was when I saw her for the first time. She had gotten to class early the way I had. I wondered if she was as nervous as I was. She looked at me as I sat on the floor next to the auditorium door. We made eye contact, and she gave me a sweet smile as she sat on the other side of the door on the ground. She had a beauty that may have been modest to most, but I thought she was stunning. Her simple, muted, medium-length hair hung close to her sharp jawline, and she wore a plain silver cuff bracelet on her wrist.

I had headphones in but took them out when she sat down. I kept awkwardly glancing in her direction, but she was focused on a book she was reading. To try to start a conversation about it, I tried to see the title, but it was nestled between her crossed legs. I opened my mouth to speak to her, but then the doors to the auditorium opened. She quickly stood up and rushed in before I had a chance to even ask her name.

And that was how it was for the first semester of college. Every day, we would both get to class early and smile at each other, but she always rushed into the auditorium before I could muster up the courage to say anything. Even during class, I would hang on to her every word while she performed monologues, but I just couldn't say anything to her. I wanted to, but her demeanor was intimidating. She was too perfect. She made me nervous—my heart would race, and my whole body would sweat. I'd think about talking to her, and my throat would dry up. I had almost given up completely on the prospect of speaking to her until we were randomly assigned to each other as partners for a group project, and we finally spoke.

"Hi," she said to me at the end of class.

My heart fluttered. Her voice was so soft and airy. She had such a strong voice on stage. It contrasted with her everyday speaking voice, which I hadn't heard until then.

"Hi," I said, almost shaking from nerves. "My name is Knor."

"I know," she said with a smile. "I'm Sally."

We stood there for a few seconds in silence. But surprisingly, it wasn't awkward. She let out a small giggle. "I guess we should exchange numbers?"

That was the true beginning of our love story. Being around her made me feel calm in a way I wasn't used to, which meant a lot to me because I was a pretty anxious person. Even thinking about first talking to her made me feel on edge. But once I finally did, all the anxiety melted away.

Our time together was wonderful. We talked about the things we loved and had in common. We both liked being out in nature and watching movies and of course acting. We laughed about funny stories from our past such as when I tried to walk across a frozen lake and it cracked on me halfway through causing me to fall straight in. Sally's laugh was indescribable and addicting. After I heard it once, I wanted to make her laugh forever.

But sometimes we even cried a little. We had both lost people we loved, such as me with my mom and Sally, who had lost both her parents. But we also remembered the good stories, although they also made us cry.

We barely passed the group project because we couldn't stop talking about life when we were together. And we spent every free moment with each other. We would stay up for hours at night, sharing memories and dreams. She had done a lot of traveling, and I would listen to her fascinating tales. And she would listen to all my stories about my first degree and my past ambitions, such as when I wanted to be president.

We moved in together a year later, and I proposed at midnight on January first of our last semester of college. Luckily, she said yes.

We hadn't started planning the wedding officially yet, but we had some ideas of what we wanted to do. Of course, we were poor college students who were about to try to break into acting careers, so we didn't have much money. We weren't thinking of anything extravagant. We were just happy to be sharing our life together.

That was what made it so painful to deal with her lying to me the whole time. I thought she was the only person who would never be dishonest to me, but in fact, she had told the worst and most intricate lie I could have ever imagined.

As I stood in front of her in our new reality on the spaceship, I was in even more disbelief—I didn't even think that was possible.

"What did you say?" I asked.

"I'm dying," she said again.

Nausea filled my stomach. I leaned forward, crossed my arms on the table, and rested my head on them. Tears started filling my eyes. Two things kept swirling through my head. First, the love of my life was dying. I didn't know how much longer I had with her, and I wanted to cherish every single moment. Even though I was still mad at her for lying, the news made me temporarily forget that anger.

Second, which was a selfish thing, I kept thinking, not only am I the last human alive, but the only other person I know is going to abandon me and leave me alone in this galaxy. I lifted my head up, a few tears streaming down. She gave me a sad smile filled with pity.

"Are you sick?" I asked

"No," she started, "I'm not sick. But my heart has stopped beating."

"What?" I shouted. "Like right now? Did your heart just stop beating?"

Tierly reached across the table and put her hands on my arm. "No, no, no," she said quickly before I could get any more wound up. "It stopped a couple of years ago. It takes a long time for my species to die after our hearts stop. I still have a while before it kills me. Many more years. But that's why Sayrah and Talents were so mad. I knew, and I hadn't told them, so that's one reason they're angry with me. They are also very young for Links. Maybe around eighteen in Link years, which is hundreds in human years. Still, particularly Saryah can be extra emotional."

I looked again at Tierly's hand on my arm. I still wasn't sure how I felt about her touching me. But right then, it didn't feel wrong. As soon as she saw me looking at her hand, though, she moved it.

"Remember when I was really upset and told you I had lost one of my scholarships?" she asked. I nodded, tears drying up in my eyes. "That's when my heart stopped."

I remembered that vividly. It was one of the things that made me want to be with her. She was so distraught, but she'd handled it so gracefully.

I couldn't understand how someone could survive after their heart stopped. But I had a more important question on my mind. "What were you doing on Earth?" I asked as I pushed away my noodles. I had lost my appetite.

"Well…" She paused. "Honestly, we were there just out of curiosity. We had visited many years before and just wanted to see how your species had progressed. So Talents, Sayrah, and I decided to spend a few years exploring Earth. I had spent a couple of years traveling the world, and I had just arrived in the US when I met you. I knew you were special, but I tried to keep my distance.

"But after months of not talking to you and then being assigned that project together, I couldn't help but fall in love with you. This brings me to another point; Talents and Sayrah were also mad at me because I had decided to be with you. They were off doing their own thing while you and I were together. I hadn't talked to them in a couple of years. But they were coming to the US for my graduation, and I was going to introduce you to them. They still would've been mad because we technically have a rule about not dating when we visit other planets. But once my heart stopped, I decided it didn't matter anymore."

I pondered what she said for a moment. Her statements only raised more questions, but I did have an overwhelming feeling of love for her again. I didn't want her to die. Even if she said, she had many more years. What if she was just saying that to appease me? But I couldn't think about that. I needed to focus.

"So, how old are you exactly?" I asked. She said she had been to Earth "many years before," but I didn't know what that meant. Before that moment, I thought Tierly was twenty-four. But at that point, I knew she had to be much older.

Tierly laughed and shook her head. "I can't tell you."

"Why not?" I protested.

"Because," she said, "I'm so old that you can't comprehend it. Just know when I came to Earth the first time, humans, as you know them now, were still evolving."

Still evolving? How could she be that old? That was tens of thousands of years. No wonder she could've gone a couple of years without talking to Talents and Sayrah. A year must've been nothing to her.

But then an interesting question came to mind. "Do you know why my planet was destroyed?" After I asked, I realized she probably wouldn't know.

But to my surprise, after a small pause, she answered, "I do. You were attacked by Zyeens. It's a hive species that has run out of resources on their planet, so they've been traveling the universe looking for planets with specific metals that they use to build ships and expand their empire.

"I haven't always lived in Maltina. The Links with us now moved there years ago after my planet was destroyed by the Zyeens. I was younger at the time and could create a much larger forcefield, so I saved most of my species. But our planet was destroyed, and we had to leave immediately to get away from the Zyeens. We traveled for a few years before we landed on Maltina and colonized it. My species is far more advanced than the Zyeens, but there are very few of us, so we can't compete with their numbers. There are millions of those ships that attacked your planet and thousands of Zyeens on each one. My species is only a few hundred."

I thought for a moment about what she had said. It was a lot to process. But I asked my most persistent question. "What is a hive species?"

"A hive species is one that is all connected mentally and controlled by a queen," she stated. "Their main goal in life is simply to expand and become larger. That's why they need metals from Earth to build more ships and colonize them. However, there's another reason they destroy all life forms; once they see a species developing in science, particularly space expedition, they feel threatened. So they destroy the species entirely. They've tried to do that to my species, but like I said, we were able to escape."

"Oh…" I said again. I understood what she was saying, but it didn't make sense how any species would feel the need to eradicate another. But then I thought of Earth and humans and all the times my own species had tried to wipe out another race simply because of their skin color or religious beliefs. I supposed if my species was like that, it wasn't hard to imagine that others would feel the same way.

"There is another reason the Zyeens attacked us…" she said suspiciously.

"Oh ok," I started. "Why?"

Tierly let out a large sigh. "They.. well that eat us."

My eyes widened. "What?!"

"Yeah, they believe our ashes are I guess… magical because we each have a few powers," she said almost awkwardly. "So they destroy our planet by burning it and they scavenge the ashes and cook with them. At least they give it to their queen."

I didn't have long to think about that before we were interrupted. Tierly, who was facing the door, suddenly had an urgent look in her eyes as she stared past me. I turned around quickly and saw Sayrah's head poking around the corner with a frown on her face.

"Hey, baby," Tierly said as she stood up.

I sat awkwardly in my chair, looking slowly back and forth between Tierly and Sayrah. Did Tierly call Sayrah "baby"?

"Ugh, never mind," Sayrah said. "I'm not hungry anymore." And with that, she walked back out the door, but not before she whispered, "Have fun with your new family."

Chapter Nine

Instead of going back to my room to be alone, I decided to go bug Talents in the control room. The ship didn't really need a pilot, but Talents enjoyed sitting at the helm and checking on things around him. It was like how people on Earth would stare at their cell phones for hours. Talents just liked seeing how close we were or how fast we were going. He also looked up the information. At the moment, he was probably focusing on the Zyeens ships back on Earth. Just checked to make sure they weren't following us. We had an anti-tracker and cloak, but the Zyeens technology was advanced and was getting better every day. So, he was still being cautious.

"How's everything looking?" I asked Talents as I entered the room and walked behind him. He didn't answer so I asked again. "How's everything looking?"

He sighed. "You need to be nice for once in your life." He waved his hand across the control panel and the pink blanket over the window turned back into the vastness of space. Before I could retaliate, he went over the intercom, "We are about 10 minutes from Maltina." Then, he surprised me by turning toward me and giving me all his attention.

"Why should I be nice?"

"For Mother's sake."

I scoffed. I wanted to say she never thought of us, but I didn't because I knew it wasn't true. And Talents would have definitely called me out. Mother had birthed me even though there was a good chance it would kill her. But she said she knew I was going to be special and worth everything. She was also a great mother. Maybe a little too independent at times, but with how long Links live, I can't expect her to be there every second of my life. But still, I was upset.

I heard in the distance down the passageway Mother calming Knor down. I rolled my eyes while looking at Talents. He opened his mouth to speak and I just said, "Oops, forgot my pendant," and rushed out of the room.

***

I sat there for a moment while I processed everything that had just been said. Great. Not only was I going to a new planet with a new species where I only really knew one person, but the two people I barely knew were giving me the impression that they hated me. Things were gonna suck.

Sayrah abruptly left the room, and Tierly stood leaning on the wall of the doorway, looking defeated. I had some more questions to ask, but I wasn't sure if it was the right time. I decided to be empathic even though I was also mad at her. "Are you okay?" I asked as kindly as I could.

Tierly didn't turn around when I spoke to her. "It'll be okay," she said. "I hope…" She hesitated for a moment then turned back around with a sad smile.

"So, are Sayrah and Talents related to you?" All I could think about was Tierly calling Sayrah "baby." I had never heard her call anyone "baby" except me. I wondered if maybe Tierly was polyamorous and Sayrah was her wife, which didn't settle well with me. I was angry imagining Tierly having more than one partner. But my anger subsided when what she said next put me in a state of shock.

"Well… actually, Sayrah and Talents are my children," she said.

"Holy shit," I said, sounding a little more surprised than I'd planned to. I let out a nervous giggle. "I didn't think I could be any more surprised, but I was wrong." The news didn't upset me like I thought it would. The only thing I wondered was who the father was.

That made me question if Tierly had another spouse on her planet. I mean, she lied to her kids about dying, and she lied to me about—everything. Maybe she also had a partner who didn't know about me or that she was dying. So I asked, "Please just be honest with me. Do you have a boyfriend or husband I don't know about?"

Tierly gave me a confused look, but then smiled and shook her head. "No," she said plainly. "You're the only one I love."

I looked down, feeling my cheeks warm. It was going to be so hard to stay mad at her. While she stood there in her gown with her sparkling green eyes, all I could think about was how much I wanted to kiss her. But I fought the urge to go over to her. I remembered that the beautiful woman and her lavender skin had betrayed me. I couldn't trust her anymore, which was ironic because the only way I was going to survive everything was if I *did* trust her.

After a long moment, I looked up at her, and she smiled and asked, "Do you wanna change clothes?"

I looked down at my dress pants and pink striped button-up shirt. I wasn't sure exactly how long I had been on the ship, but I definitely felt like I needed to get out of those clothes. I wondered if I had to wear a gown like everyone else.

Tierly must have noticed me looking her up and down, and she laughed. "You don't have to wear a dress." She motioned for me to follow her. I felt strange leaving my half-eaten food on the table, but I got up and followed her. We drifted through the false wall that connected to the other passageway and walked over to my room. She entered first, but I wasn't far behind. I felt a twinge of satisfaction when I noticed the symbols on the wall had meaning, just as they had in the other rooms. I could see one that said Shower another that read Clothes and a third that I was really excited about, a symbol that said Bed.

I looked at the strange tub filled with jelly that I had woken up in.

I wondered why they had a symbol for a bed but also had a tub to sleep in. Tierly answered my question before I had a chance to ask.

"The hibernation tub is a good place to sleep and heal," she said. "I put you in there just in case you had some damage from the smoke inhalation on Earth. You seemed fine, but after you passed out a couple of times, I just wanted to be sure."

"So why do you have a Bed symbol if you can just sleep in the… hibernation tub?" I asked.

Tierly started blushing. I wasn't sure why or what I had said to make her blush. But she smiled and said, "I added the bed option to this room and my room after we started dating. Just in case you were ever on the ship, I wanted to be able to sleep in the same bed with you. That was something I really enjoyed about human culture, sleeping in the same space."

The only thing I could think about was how she thought she might have brought me on her ship. She was basically saying she had the intention to tell me the truth. That brought me a little comfort and made me even less angry at her.

I looked at the Clothes symbol on the wall. I wondered if it worked like the food dispenser. I walked over to the symbol, lifted my hand, and looked at Tierly. She gave me a nod, and I placed my hand on the symbol, thinking about a pair of workout shorts, boxers, and a T-shirt. What I thought was going to happen was a compartment would appear, and I would take out the clothes. But instead, a light quickly flashed over me. I stepped back, trying to avoid it, but it went over me so quickly I couldn't stop it, and suddenly, I had on black-and-red workout shorts, a pair of snug boxers, and a perfectly fitted white T-shirt.

"Comfortable?" Tierly asked.

"Huh," I said, amused. It was all I could think to say. Although I would much rather have had my planet back, so far, the new, advanced technology has been very interesting.

Before I could ask her how it worked, Talents made an announcement through what I guessed was some kind of ship intercom. "We're about ten minutes from Maltina."

For a small amount of time, I had been relaxed. Tierly and I had talked, I got some food, changed my clothes, and learned a few new things. But at that moment, I was about to have a heart attack. For a second, I couldn't breathe. I clutched my hand to my chest and started hyperventilating. Tierly ran over to me and put one hand on my shoulder and another on my chest. The walls started spinning.

"Hey, hey, hey," Tierly said empathetically. "It's okay. It's okay. I promise."

I looked at her, fear overcoming my body and mind. I had problems with panic attacks. And of course, I didn't have any medicines with me. They were all on Earth. But luckily there was so much comfort in her eyes. A few tears rolled down my face.

She whispered, "Things will be strange at first, but I promise it won't be bad. You'll love Maltina, and the people there will love you too. And I'll be right beside you the whole time. I know I'm probably not your favorite person right now, but I won't let anything happen to you."

I looked around the small room. I needed air, but I was on a spaceship with no windows. Then I remembered the control room was mostly a window. Maybe that would calm my nerves. So I asked in between gasps, "Can… we… go… to… the… control room?"

Tierly smiled and said, "Of course." She pulled my hand away from my chest and led me through the door, down the passageway. I didn't see the soft pink light even though the door to the control room was still open. We made our way inside, and in front of me, through the clear window, was a cloud-covered yellow planet. The clouds were so thick you couldn't see the surface.

I took a couple of deep breaths and was able to calm down.

"It's all clouds," I said, mostly to myself.

"That's the false atmosphere," Talents chimed in. "The sun is able to get through. There's an artificial barrier below the false clouds. That creates the atmosphere we live in."

I looked at the planet in awe. I didn't understand how their technology worked or how it was so advanced. But Tierly did say she was thousands of years old, so I supposed she probably had learned a lot in her lifetime.

I suddenly became very curious. The dread and anxiety were still there, but I was also wildly excited. My life had transformed so much in only a day or so. I still mourned for my friends and family and likely would for years to come, but my life was about to completely change.

We got closer and closer to the planet until the ship quickly disappeared into the clouds, and I nearly fell as the atmosphere rushed across the control room window. It only took about three seconds of being in the thick yellow clouds before we burst through, and my jaw dropped. All of a sudden, there was a grid-like structure that rested below the yellow clouds. I was almost scared, remembering the grid structure of ships that had attacked Earth. But as we got closer, I noticed it was that same sleek black material that covered the walls of the ship. We paused for a moment, floating above the metal. Talents moved his hands methodically over the water's surface, and a small opening appeared in the glossy metal.

I looked momentarily at Talents; out of the corner of my eye, I saw a symbol pop up on the control panel that read "error." I was concerned for a moment, but Talents simply brushed it away. I was going to ask him if everything was okay, but then I saw through the hole in the metal grid.

As we made our way through the opening, below us was a beautiful green landmass with sporadic white clouds floating gently through the clear air and a bright blue ocean. It was breathtaking. The closer we got, the more I could see a large forest, and in the middle was a clearing. I saw many small ships that I assumed were identical to the one we were in. We flew above a little opening in the field of ships, immediately started to drop, and finally landed.

Talents stood up from his chair, which suddenly disappeared. He walked over to Tierly and me as we stood near the window. An endless row of ships appeared through the glass. I expected to be led somewhere before exiting the ship. But as soon as Talents walked up, the whole window vanished, and I felt a warm breeze across my skin. The air smelled of pine trees and cinnamon, almost like Christmas. Then a metal walkway appeared, leading to the ground just outside the window.

Before we even had a chance to step out, Sayrah came barreling through, almost pushing Talents down. "Hey!" he shouted. "I'm not the one you're mad at. Jeez…"

She stomped her way down the ramp and disappeared into the woods to our left. I was hesitant to step on the ramp. It was that same smooth black metal that was all over the ship. I was worried I'd either fall through or slip. But Talents gave me a smile and made his way down the gradually declining ramp to the sand and grass below.

"Follow me," Tierly said as she started descending the ramp.

I looked cautiously at it and finally took a step. It supported my weight, so I took another. I was completely outside of the ship, breathing in the fresh warm air. Before I could even change my mind and turn around to escape back inside, the window closed. I turned around in a panic and put my hands desperately on the glass, but it didn't open.

Tierly came and placed her hand on my shoulder. "I told you; you'll be fine. Just follow me."

I hesitantly turned back around, got my nerves under control, and walked all the way down the ramp. Tierly had gone to the left, and in front of her was a thick forest. I thought I was going to need a machete to get through, but as soon as she stepped closer to the wooded area, the trees and bushes moved, and a pathway appeared.

"Whoa," I said aloud as I slowly made my way beside Tierly. I stared up at the tall trees of the moving forest. I looked down the pathway and saw an opening maybe one hundred feet through the trees.

"Come on," Tierly said. "I'll lead the way." She stepped into the forest, pausing to see if I was behind her. I looked at the sea of spaceships and realized I only had one choice—enter the woods and see where it led me. So I did. I walked up to Tierly, and she continued through the greenery. I kept close to her as we walked through. The trees felt alive. They creaked and moaned like a porch swing that needed oil. All the leaves moved with the faint wind that flowed through the woods. I didn't see any animals or bugs, but maybe the moving forest caused them to scatter.

I stopped for a moment to look behind me. Immediately, my chest tightened and my hands shook. The forest behind me had closed. There was no longer a pathway leading to the ships. I turned back around to tell Tierly we were trapped, but she had stopped and was looking at me. "It's okay," she said for the hundredth time. "Come on. We're almost through."

I quickly caught up to her and followed her down the path. We were just about to reach the opening. Light shone through. A tall cliff covered in large metal squares loomed ahead. Tierly turned to me, ushered me through the opening, smiled, and said, "Welcome to your new home."

Chapter Ten

I stared for a second from the passageway entrance as Talents, Mother, and Knor looked out at the trees. I felt like rolling my eyes, but I had done that so many times today. But there was just so much stupidity going on today.

As soon as the window opened and the ramp was down, I rushed past everyone. Talents yelled something at me, but I wasn't listening. I made my way through the short forest, to the sandy beaches, and up the ladder to my bungalow. Or my family's bungalow. Talents, Mother and I all lived in the same one. And, I guess, now Knor.

The thought gave me anger and goosebumps.

Not one person called to me as I walked past them to my home. But I heard them all shout "Talents" as he walked close behind me. He greeted everyone quickly but continued to follow me.

"Stop!" he shouted as I tried to escape inside my room. As the door was closing, he stuck his foot in a small crack and the door opened back up. "We need to talk."

"No, we don't," I said as I reached for my pendant. I opened it up to a tablet and pulled up a book I liked as I laid my bed out and laid myself down. But Talents was relentless.

"I'm normally very patient with you," he started. I acted like I wasn't listening. "But you need to grow up for once. Knor is our family now. You need to accept that. You have to share Mother, which I know you hate doing."

"It's not that," I said as I laid my pendant on my chest. I closed my eyes, wishing for the days when it was just me, Talents, and Mother traveling the universe, exploring new worlds, and finding galaxies for the heart of the ship. "She's dying."

Talents and I were silent for a moment. We both didn't know what to say. But I spoke up. "She found out she was dying after only a week of our stay on Earth. She could have died at any moment and she didn't want to spend it with us. And now, here we are, back in Maltina and he is here. So once again, we won't get to spend her last days with just us."

"Just because she wants some romantic love in her last years doesn't make her a bad person."

"You don't understand," I said quietly. "If the Zyeens had never attacked, we may have never seen Mother again. She would have died without telling us. And that's something I don't know if I can forgive."

***

The warm sun beamed on my face. It blinded me for a moment as I stepped out of the forest, but my eyes quickly adjusted. Thin wispy clouds floated above, and the almost clear grid shimmered in the sky. Below me was soft sand. To my right, the tree line extended far off into the distance, and to my left, it stretched out until it reached a lake. Wooden canoes were spread across the shore where the still water rested. The most amazing thing was the towering cliff of red rock that stood about thirty stories high in front of me across the football-field-sized expanse of sand.

Looking at the cliff made my palms sweat. A grid of square metal objects covered the side of it, reminding me of the objects that destroyed Earth. I took a step back, but Tierly put her hand on my shoulder. "Those are our homes," she said.

I guessed she'd noticed me staring. But before I could speak, I spotted the people.

At first, I looked to my right and saw people coming out of the forest further down. Then, I looked at the lake and noticed five children playing on the shore. Everyone was wearing those plain cotton gowns, although they varied in color. All of the people had long hair, all different shades of red and black, and everyone's skin was a different hue of purple; some were very dark, while others were light. Although Tierly's lavender-colored skin was the lightest that I had seen so far.

I caught sight of Sayrah. She was far ahead and right next to the cliff in front of me across the sand, Talents trailing behind her. Suddenly, a blue light appeared under her and lifted her up the side of the cliff, stopping near the top beside one of the metal homes. She stepped off and disappeared into one of the homes. Unfortunately, along with my fear of needles, I was also scared of heights. I thought of what Tierly had said about the structures being their homes. I wasn't looking forward to living on a cliff. I wondered if maybe there were some homes in the forest I could live in, or if we could live on the bottom level that had direct access from the sand to the home.

While I was watching Sayrah, I didn't notice the small children coming over to me and was taken aback when a small, purple-skinned, redheaded girl with a short haircut grabbed my hand.

"You're beautiful," the little girl said.

I felt my cheeks get hot. That was something Tierly always said to me. Most people on Earth called guys handsome and girls beautiful, but Tierly always said beautiful was a stronger word.

"My name is Quesa. You must be Knor," she said with a smile.

I was caught off guard that she knew my name. I looked at Tierly, but the little girl answered. "Talents sent a message to everyone here while you were on the ship," she stated. "I'm sorry about your planet," little Quesa said while she took my hand and kissed it.

I suddenly became very sad, and a few tears threatened to fall as I thought about my family. I wished so much that I could give them one last kiss, wished I could share this experience with them.

"Oh, don't cry. This is a happy place. Just don't go into the forest at night," she whispered.

The tears stopped forming, and I looked back at the forest. I wondered what happened at night. I took a step farther out onto the sand, but as I did, I ran into someone.

"Sorry," I said, turning around. Luckily, I'd only run into Tierly. But it wasn't just her and the children anymore; it was at least twenty people. I had no idea where they had come from. For a moment, I was overwhelmed. But quickly, I realized they hadn't come to greet me. They had come to greet Tierly. Even the kids had lost interest in me. Everyone was saying, "Hello, Mother," and holding her hands and kissing them. Tierly responded to all of them saying, "Hello, my loves."

I was so confused. Were *all* those people her children? It felt a little ignorant to say, but they did all look similar. Tierly probably thought that about humans. In any event, the people were so excited to see Tierly. They hadn't greeted Talents or Sayrah that way, and I assumed they had been gone the same amount of time.

However, after everyone had a chance to greet Tierly, they directed their attention to me. At that moment, I was definitely overwhelmed. Everyone wanted to touch me. But the strangest thing was that when their hands made contact, I felt a small shock. It wasn't painful. More like a soft tickle. But as soon as the shock happened, I knew the name of the person who had touched me. It was incredible. I looked at Tierly with what I was sure was a stunned expression on my face.

She simply said, "I know. They're all saying hello. It's called a whisper. They're trying to welcome you by choosing to show you their memories. They are showing you their hearts, love, and kindness."

Suddenly, images flooded my mind. I saw each person growing

up. All of the happy memories of those different people were becoming ingrained in my mind.

Quesa touched me again, and I felt the familiar spark. I saw her playing on the shore of the lake, and I experienced the happiness she felt when she saw Tierly and me. The love the people had for Tierly was overwhelming. She was their cherished leader. And because she loved me, they all loved me too. Even though they didn't know me. I, once again, thought of my family and how I wished they could experience the feeling of welcome and love. My eyes started to water. I was about to break down in front of these people. But since I basically knew them, I didn't feel as embarrassed.

Before the tears started to flow, Tierly took my hand and said, "Okay, let's give him some space. We're going to my bungalow. We'll see you for the feast."

Tierly led me through the crowd, which looked like it had grown to forty people. I hadn't connected with all of them, but I was already content. Tierly was right. The people would love me, and I had already felt it. The love they held for me could never compare to the amount they had for Tierly, but it made me warm inside. Even after such a short amount of time in Maltina, I already felt like I had a family again.

We made it to the cliff and to what looked like a ladder. It reached all the way up to the top of the cliff, but as I looked around and saw a few people going to their homes, I noticed no one used the rungs. They simply stood right next to the ladder and were lifted into the air.

Tierly looked at me and said calmly, "You are, once again, not going to like this."

I glanced up the ladder; it went so high up, and there was no safety gear at all. I grimaced. "There don't happen to be any homes in the forest, are there?" I asked hopefully.

Tierly laughed. "I'm sorry to say, there aren't," she said. "And also, you don't wanna go in the woods at night."

I looked at her for a moment. That was the second time someone had said that. "Why can't we go into the forest at night?"

"Well… it's just not safe. I'll tell you about it tonight." Then she focused her attention back on the ladder.

I looked to my left and to my right. People were coming and going from the cliff, standing near the other ladders and being either lifted up or brought down. They acted like it was nothing. But it wasn't nothing to me. I started to shake a little. *Please let Tierly's home be near the bottom*, I thought.

"All right, all you have to do is step right here"—she motioned to a place right next to the ladder—"and think about where you wanna go, and it'll take you there."

I looked at her nervously. "But I don't know where I'm going."

Tierly looked up and pointed. "You're going all the way to the top," she said.

I gulped. My body trembled. Of course, we were going to the top. "Can we go up together?" I asked hopefully.

"No. You have to go alone."

My heart sank. I looked up again. I just didn't know if I could do it. Not only was I going up so high, but also, I didn't know if I could trust the integrity of the structures. They were small metal squares that jutted out of the cliff. I was worried they wouldn't support my weight.

It seemed like Tierly was getting tired of waiting, so she went past me, right next to the ladder, and said, "Just think about me, and it will take you to the top."

A bright blue light surrounded her, and she quickly rose up the ladder. I watched her float the entire way up until she reached the top.

She stepped to the right onto the roof of one of the homes. She looked down, which made me nervous that she was going to fall, but she simply waved for me to come up.

I took a deep breath, my body still trembling. *You got this*, I thought. I mustered up all the courage I had left, stepped right in front of the ladder, closed my eyes, and thought about Tierly. I felt a rush of air flowing all around me, but before I could think about anything else, it stopped.

I opened my eyes and stared at the cliff in front of me. I stayed frozen, unable to move or breathe. I glanced up slightly and could see the edge of the top of the cliff. I couldn't believe I was already at the top, but that made me even more fearful. I felt a hand touch my shoulder. I nearly jumped, but I thought if I moved, I would die. I realized it was Tierly, of course. I hadn't thought about what I was going to do when I got to the house. I honestly hadn't thought I would make it. I assumed something terrible would happen along the way, like falling or the ladder disappearing.

But Tierly's hand moved down to my arm, and she grabbed my hand. "Just take a step toward me," she said in a soothing tone. "It will be okay. Now focus. See what you want, not what you fear. You are stronger than your fears and anxieties. I promise."

I continued to stare at the ominous cliff and wondered how long the blue light would hold me. I quickly looked over at Tierly and made the mistake of looking down. But before I could scream or panic, Tierly pulled me onto the metal square she was standing on. I was reminded of how strong she was. However, I didn't have any relief standing on the metal. There were no railings to keep me from falling. I immediately slammed my body against the cliff and started freaking out. The metal square was only about ten feet in front of me and five feet on either side. I looked up. We were almost at the top of the cliff; I could nearly reach my hand up and touch it. I spread my arms out and held onto whatever part of the cliff I could grab. I tried so hard to listen to the words she had said, *See what you want, not what you fear*." But it was so hard.

Tierly, however, looked very calm. She walked from the edge of the metal bungalow to a spot right in front of me. She squatted down and placed her hand on the metal. A small opening appeared, and Tierly reached her hand up toward me. I looked in the hole. There was a ladder. I grabbed Tierly's hand and stepped onto the top rung and made my way down. It was a good ten feet. I wondered how Talents had jumped so far without getting hurt.

The surroundings in the metal bungalow were similar to the ship. There was a small room covered in sleek glowing black material with four words spread out that said Door Controls. I wondered where the doors could go considering the room looked about as big as the whole structure. Tierly jumped down beside me and walked over to the first door on the left. She pushed the symbol twice, and the door opened. We both walked in, but I was shocked at what I saw.

It was a huge octagonal-shaped room that was much more colorful than the rooms on the ship. Plum and crimson tapestries covered the walls on my side, and intricate emerald and lapis rugs covered the floor. It was an odd color combination, but the darkness created a comfort about them. It was like the end of a richly colored rainbow. The colors and thick fabrics absorbed the little bit of light in the room.

About twenty feet in front of me was a huge tinted window that looked out over the sand and forest below us. There was a beautiful antique-looking couch that sat facing the window. I imagined her spending hours sitting there thinking about the universe. It was very peaceful.

As Tierly walked farther into the room, it started to glow. It was dim, but enough to see everything. The window was tinted, but there was still a decent amount of light coming through. She went over to the couch, sat down, and motioned for me to join her. I hesitated at first because the couch was close to the window, and I was still dazed that I was up that high. But she seemed so relaxed that I slowly made my way over, though every step was cautious. I made it to the couch and sat. I was curious as to what was in the other three rooms and if they were all so big.

I looked around the room at all the colorful deep tapestries. They had all different types of patterns. Some were gentle and elegant with swirls and ocean waves, while others were strong and harsh with jagged lines and sharp mountains. But they were all beautiful.

As I was sitting, I decided to get comfortable. So I took off my shoes and let out a sigh. After sitting and relaxing for a moment, I was overcome with exhaustion. I leaned back onto the couch and closed my eyes. I figured I would lie there for a moment and then ask her to show me the other rooms. But instead, I fell asleep.

Chapter Eleven

I heard a strange noise while I was sitting in my room reading on my pendant. At first, I heard Mother and Knor arrive. I was a little sad I missed him getting to our bungalow. I had heard he was scared of heights and lucky for him, our home was right near the top of the cliff. I would have liked to have watched him squirm.

The noise, however, was a familiar one in a way. It was someone snoring. Talents was known for his wallpaper-ripping snore, but the sound wasn't him. I thought that it couldn't be someone snoring because Mother and Knor had just gotten to the bungalow. I wondered if maybe it was Talents.

I tried to ignore it and keep reading my story, but it was too distracting. I turned my pendant back into its pebble-sized form and grunted as I made my way off my bed, which disappeared as soon as I got off.

It wasn't long till I made my way into the common room or den where I heard the snoring coming from. I burst through the door, and opened my mouth to speak, but quickly heard an "Shhhhhh!" come from the couch. I choke on my halted breath. Mother was looking at me suspiciously. She pointed to the other end of the couch where Knor lay sleeping, but not quietly. I wanted to scream real loud to scare him and wake him up, but then I saw her and how she looked at him. Her head was slightly tilted and she had the biggest grin I'd ever seen, as if she had waited for this moment, but wasn't sure if it would ever happen.

I sighed. I was conflicted. I couldn't decide if I should try to break them up, or just let her be happy. But the decision was simple. I love Mother and, if this man really made her happy, I guess I should accept it. It doesn't mean I would be happy about it or even nice to him, but I decided I wouldn't try to break them up.

Mother stood up and walked over to me. Talents came in the room at the same time and Mother motioned for him to be quiet, which he immediately saw, and heard, Knor snoring. Mother motioned for both of us to go out of the room, so we did.

"Can't he sleep in his own room?" I asked with a scowl.

"Just let him be," Mother said sweetly. "Are you both still mad at me?"

Talents and I spoke at the same time. My answer was yes but he was no. I glared at him, although I already knew he wasn't mad anymore.

"I'm so sorry," Mother started, "to the both of you. I should have told you my heart had stopped. I just… I think I was scared. If I told anyone it would become real. Especially if I told you two. And then with Knor… I don't know. I've just been under this spell since I met him. He's all I can think about. Once I met him, I kind of forgot about my real life and was so ready to spend the rest of mine with him."

"So, is that supposed to make us feel better?" I asked. "You are still saying you would rather have spent the rest of your life with someone other than your two children. Don't you see how terrible that is?... Ugh, never mind. I'm gonna go to the beach."

I bolted out the door up to the roof and quickly made my way down the ladder to sit on the sand with my feet in the water. I wasn't sure if Mother would ever understand how much she had hurt me.

***

As I slumbered deeply on the couch, my mind was filled with the memories of the people of Maltina—memories from events in their lives happening from their perspective. I picked up that the people didn't originate from Maltina, just as Tierly had told me. They all seemed to come from different planets and of different species. They all had a similar memory of being taken away from their original planet, but I couldn't figure out why.

The dreams started with the Links leaving their homes and coming to Maltina. But as they were leaving, I saw many different species. Some of them had long soft tentacles, while others had broad sharp features. All were of varying sizes and colors. At first, the dreams were mostly sad; the young aliens were getting removed from their homes as young children and forced to live on another planet. Then the dreams shifted, and they were happy, young children playing on Maltina, gleeful and content. But then, my own mind started taking over the dreams, which quickly turned into nightmares.

I was wandering through the forest at night, lost and unable to find my way out. The trees started closing in on me, and in every opening of the forest I ran to, a strange alien species would be waiting for me. They came after me as their oddly shaped faces morphed into terrifying, deformed, demon-like apparitions with blood dripping down and tentacles jutting out of their heads.

Just before I had reached the final opening in the forest and all of the monsters from my dream were about to catch me, I heard someone call my name. Out of nowhere, Tierly appeared in my dream. "Hey!" she said forcefully as she grabbed my face. "Wake up!"

In an instant, I sat up, awakening from my place on the couch with my heart pounding, unable to catch my breath. I felt something on me, and I quickly thrashed to get it off; it was a blanket. Tierly reached her hand out and placed it gently on my shoulder. "Hey," she said in a much calmer tone. "Sorry, I didn't realize you were having such a bad dream, or I would have woken you up sooner. I've been cooking. Are you hungry?"

It took me a moment to gain my composure and process what she'd said. But I looked around the room, surrounded by beautiful tapestries, and saw Talents sitting in a chair on one side of the room staring at me with a concerned look. I wondered how long he had been there.

I sat up slowly and stretched out all my limbs. I felt rested even though I had slept on a couch. I looked out the large window, still hesitant by how high up I was. The sun had gone down, and there were fires all around that lit up the ground. I took a deep breath through my nose, and I smelled the most delicious smell. I could almost taste it because it was so strong. It reminded me of a combination of sweet yeast from freshly cooked bread and aromatic jasmine rice. I sniffed the air, enjoying every smell. The scents calmed me down. I looked over at Tierly and answered her question, "Yes. I'm very hungry."

"Good," she said with a smile. "It's almost time for the feast."

I wondered what she meant. I was going to ask what the feast was, but remembering how bright it was when I fell asleep, I wondered what time it was instead. "How long was I asleep?" I asked.

"About ten hours," she said plainly.

My jaw dropped. "Ten hours? You let me sleep for ten hours?!"

Tierly laughed and said, "One day on Maltina is thirty-six hours split into about thirty-minute increments. So it wasn't as long as you think."

I looked over at Talents, but he was no longer paying attention to me. He had brought out his glass tablet and was distracted. Tierly was still standing beside me.

"You've been cooking?" I asked, wondering why they didn't just eat crack noodles as they did on the ship. But whatever she cooked did smell good.

"Yes," she said. "I made some fish and grains. Are you ready to meet all the Links at the feast?"

That statement raised two questions: what did she mean by

"Links," and again, what was "the feast"? I asked, "What is a Link?"

"Ha!" She laughed. "That's what our species is called. Links. I guess I should have told you that sooner."

"Oh, okay," I said. "Then what is the feast?"

I heard a familiar scoff come from the door behind me. I turned around on the couch while Tierly and Talents focused their attention in the same direction. Sayrah was leaning through the doorway with a smirk on her face.

"Oh," Sayrah said, "Tierly didn't tell you? We brought you back here to sacrifice you to our gods and cook you after. That's what the feast is." I looked at Sayrah, unamused. Talents and Tierly did as well. "Wow… tough crowd," she said as she walked away.

I looked back at Tierly. She had a scowl on her face, but she rolled her eyes and shook her head. She said, "The feast is simply dinner. Everyone makes a dish, and we all eat together at the beach. Here in Maltina, we only eat once a day. But don't worry. I have crack noodles in the house if you're ever hungry before the feast in the evening." She gave me a playful wink.

I had many more questions, like why did all of those people—Links—have memories of being taken away from a different alien species? And how did they share memories? And how was it that the square bungalow was so small on the outside but so much larger on the inside?

Tierly gave me a concerned look. I must have looked displeased when she answered. But, really, I was just curious and thinking. She said to me, "If you don't wanna go to the feast, you don't have to. I can bring you back some food."

I considered that for a moment. I wondered how many people would be there and if they would all try to share their memories with me. That was an incredible experience, but it was very exhausting and overwhelming. I was hungry, but I wasn't sure I could handle the memories again. Sleeping ten hours didn't help because I was still tired. However, I didn't want to be rude. She said they eat together every night so, surely, they would be offended if I wasn't there.

Tierly sat down beside me on the couch. She looked at me and gave me a sympathetic smile. "Are you okay?" she asked as she placed her hand on my leg.

Suddenly, all I wanted to do was kiss her. I looked down at her hand and contemplated holding it. It was strange because I was still angry with her, but the magical side to her that I had never seen was hypnotizing. It made me feel more attracted to her, and I wanted to let go of the anger. And for the first time in a while, I wanted to be with her again. Her touch didn't make me recoil. I embraced it.

I was still overwhelmed by the desire to kiss her, so I asked a simple question. "Where will I be sleeping?"

She smiled. "You don't like the couch?" she asked humorously. She patted my leg and stood up. "Follow me."

I stood up quickly and had a big stretch, letting out a loud yawn. I glanced at Talents, who was watching me. He smiled, and we both let out a small laugh. Tierly, who was standing in the doorway, had a cute grin on her face. I walked over to her, and we both disappeared into the dim hallway area where I had first entered the bungalow. There were four doors, including the one that we'd just come out of, which was the farthest to the left. We walked to the door on the far right. "This door leads to the bedrooms," she said. "All of them. Just place your hand here, think of your room, and when the door opens it will be there." She placed her hand on the door control symbol and pushed it twice.

The door slid open, and I glanced inside. The room was large but very plain. It looked like the ones with the sleek black walls on the ship. But the room had one difference; there was a large window on the other side that overlooked the beach. There were also similar symbols on the walls of the space. Thankful again for my translators, I knew they said things like Bed, Bathroom, Clothes, and Food.

"I know this room is boring," Tierly stated. "But you can spruce it up."

On one hand, I wanted to stay there and go back to sleep. But I was hungry, so the feast would probably be a very satisfactory thing. On the other hand, I wanted to get the bed out and ravish Tierly. That was a sudden, odd feeling because deep down, I was still mad at her for lying to me, so I didn't want to be close to her. But learning everything about her new life was stimulating and erotic. I was very conflicted. It was strange to love and hate someone at the same time.

After a moment of silence standing in the doorway, Tierly said, "Why don't you just stay here and relax? I'll bring you back some food."

"No," I said, finally deciding what I was going to do. "I'd like to go to the feast, as long as what Sayrah said wasn't true."

Tierly laughed and said, "No, we aren't going to eat you."

Tierly walked out of the doorway into the hallway area, and I turned around to follow. She made her way to the other side of the small room and pushed a symbol on the wall that said Ladder. A clear ladder appeared, and a small hole opened above it. Tierly put one hand on the ladder and then looked at me.

"We have to go on the lift again," she said apprehensively.

I swallowed and looked up at the opening. I wasn't excited about going on the roof again. I wondered if I could convince her to put up a large fence on the roof so I could at least feel a little safer up there. But before I could ask, Tierly was quickly up the ladder. I wasn't happy, but I followed her.

I hesitated as my head popped up through the opening to the roof.

I let out a fearful sigh—we were so high up. I crawled my way out of the bungalow, and Tierly reached her hand out to me. I grabbed it, and she quickly lifted me up. I jumped back and glued myself to the wall of the cliff, dragging Tierly with me. She didn't expect the sudden motion; it abruptly pulled her in front of me. We were so close that I could smell her sweet perfume. Not only was my heart beating fast out of fear, but it was beating even faster because she was right next to me. The desire to kiss her returned, yet again. I could almost taste her sweet lips and feel their soft texture. I couldn't imagine anything more passionate than kissing at this terrifying moment. I thought maybe it could set off a spark between us again- but maybe that was wishful thinking. Still… I couldn't stop thinking about it.

Apparently unaffected by our physical proximity, Tierly simply laughed and walked over to the tall ladder that she called the lift. She stepped out onto what seemed to be thin air, and I flinched a little with apprehension for her even though I knew the small translucent pale-blue platform would appear under her foot. When it did, she stepped her other foot onto it and turned around to look at me. "Just think about going to the bottom," she stated. "It's just as easy as going up. You'll be fine."

Before I had a chance to say anything, the platform quickly moved, and Tierly was transported down.

It just seemed so unnatural to step out onto nothing when I was thirty stories up. But I inched my way over to the lift. I wondered if I needed to step on slowly or quickly. It probably didn't matter. I was very hesitant, but I trusted Tierly. She hadn't led me astray yet. So without looking down, I stepped into thin air, but luckily, I felt something beneath my foot. I had a slight feeling of relief, but I was still thirty stories up, so I wasn't *that* relieved. Closing my eyes, I whispered, "Take me to the ground. Take me to the ground." Suddenly, the air started to rush beside me, and my stomach was in my throat. I didn't feel nauseous, just like I was falling. But after a few seconds, the air stopped whooshing, and I was no longer moving.

I felt the sand under my feet. I remembered I had taken my shoes off and hadn't thought to put them back on. I hoped everyone wouldn't be offended that I didn't have shoes on. I hadn't really looked at Tierly's feet to see what she was wearing.

However, the warm soft cushion of sand under my feet made me feel comforted. The beach had always given me a sense of happiness: the relaxing splash of the crashing waves, and the warmth of the sun cascading across my skin. I turned around and looked at the beauty of the landscape and the small drifting waves in the dark water. I could hear them slightly, but I could barely see them in the dim firelight. I felt like walking over and putting my feet in the ocean. I loved floating in the moving water. It always relaxed me. I didn't go to the beach often, but when I did, I always left feeling refreshed. The air was a little humid and sticky, but I didn't really mind because it was mildly cool.

I glanced around. There were multiple bonfires and torches set up all around the large sand area. And the most beautiful things were the very large glass tables filled with the most delicious food I had ever seen. There were all types of cooked meats and veggies with the scents of a five-star restaurant wafting from them. All the different seasonings smelled so enticing. I couldn't tell what they were, but they made me hungry. I closed my eyes, and the aromas filled my nose with pleasure; I could basically taste everything.

All the people sitting at the tables talking. No one was eating yet though. A few people noticed me and gave me a big smile. But the biggest smile I got was from little Quesa who was sitting at the middle of the table, waving frantically at me. She was almost standing on the table trying to get my attention. I gave her a huge grin and a small wave. I noticed Tierly was standing to my left waiting for me. I took a few hesitant steps toward her and then immediately felt the wind from someone coming down the ladder right behind me. I jumped and turned around in fear only to see Talents, still staring at his glass tablet. He walked past me and found a place at one of the tables. I heard a few giggles from the people who were watching me. Quesa let out a big laugh.

I went and stood next to Tierly, and she motioned for me to follow her. We walked all the way to the end of the largest table. As we walked closer and closer to the edge of the forest, I became nervous. I tried to shake it off. Tierly wouldn't put me in danger. But I had more than once not to go into the forest at night. I decided to log that question for later.

Tierly went all the way to the end of the table where two small glass chairs were waiting. She looked at me and said, "These spots are for us. Have a seat."

I looked at the chairs. It was weird because we were at the head of the table. On Earth, normally, that was a leader's or host's position. I didn't feel like either. But then I noticed the silence and felt the eyes on me. I looked down the long table and saw every single face looking at me.

I suddenly became self-conscious. I was so different from those people. They all had different shades of beautiful purple skin. They all wore simple cotton gowns. Their eyes glowed in the candlelight. And there I was. Some weird human with dark-brown skin, wearing workout shorts and a T-shirt. I wondered what they thought of me. And then I remembered all the sweet, accepting feelings some of them had shared with me when I first got there. I hoped they all were that welcoming; they were all smiling, so I told myself it was possible. I looked at Tierly, and she was still motioning for me to sit down. So I did.

Tierly walked over to her chair and stood behind it. She put her hand on my shoulder and said, "We now have a new member of our family. I know Talents already told you, and some of you have already connected with him, but this is Knor. I know you'll all treat him with respect and kindness."

I looked down at the table while Tierly was speaking, and I caught Sayrah's reaction. She rolled her eyes and leaned back, appearing frustrated after she caught my gaze. I wondered what it was about me she didn't like and why she had no problem wearing her emotions on her sleeves.

Then Tierly sat down as everyone continued staring at her and me. She raised her hands and said, "Now, let's begin."

Chapter Twelve

I stared down at Knor. We had made eye contact during Mother's speech. I hoped I didn't make him feel comfortable.

I wanted to laugh as he looked at the table. He obviously didn't know what to do. Everyone was filling their plates, while he just sat there. I thought for a very brief moment that I should help him. But that intrusive thought didn't last long. Besides, Talents was going over to him.

I snatched a pickle of fruit and got up from the table. Nobody seemed to notice when I left. I walked over to the forest.

The Links were all incredibly nice to me, but even them I didn't like very much. I supposed they liked me, although I'm not sure why. Quesa was always in my face when I was trying to relax. It had been nice to get away for a few years on Earth. I could sit at a coffee shop, and no one would bother me. On Maltina, someone always wanted to talk.

As I approached the edge of the forest, I had a naughty idea.

I looked at the forest and then up at the sky. The sun had completely gone, which meant the forest was not a safe place. There were a few creatures that roamed in there at night, which we called Ancestors. Most of the time, they stayed away from the edge of the forest and kept to the middle. But I wondered… they do have an agonizing scream. If I could find a way to instigate them, I bet Knor would be terrified.

I was pleased with my idea. And I knew how to attract them to the edge of the forest.

I peeked back at the table: no one was paying attention to me, so I cloaked and made myself invisible after I put my glasses on and turned my pendant into a tablet. Luckily the Ancestors have an incredible sense of smell so they didn't need to see me.

I scanned the dark forest and saw the information pop up in front of me. There was one not too far from me. So, I stuck my arm past the forcefield into the forest and waited anxiously while looking carefully at my tablet. It wasn't long before one of them caught the smell of my blood and came rushing over to me. I timed it perfectly when I moved my arm back out of the forest just as the Ancestor was about to grab it.

I ran back over to the table uncloaked myself, and sat back down.

All that was left to do was wait.

***

At first, I was nervous. The large group of Links all started eating, but I didn't recognize any of the foods. There were some that were gray or dark reddish that I assumed were meats, and there were vibrant multicolored dishes that I thought might be fruits and vegetables. Maybe the strange brown squiggles were a type of noodle? I was hesitant to eat, but everyone was digging in. Tierly was turned away from me talking to a Link woman next to us. I didn't want to interrupt, but I had a strange fear that I shouldn't eat the delicious-looking and amazing-smelling foods. But just as I was about to give up and wait to eat some crack noodles, Talents came and sat by me.

"Here," he said as he held a strange-looking pink fruit. It had some dark pink nubs coming out of it and was about the size of a tennis ball but curved. He split it in two and handed half of it to me. I took it from him and looked at it suspiciously. The inside was actually a dark green color, and there were tiny black seeds. I stared at it for a moment, unsure how to eat it. Talents took his half tapped it against mine and said, "Cheers." He took one big bite, skin and all, and then made a face as if he had taken a shot of liquor. I laughed and almost put mine down, but he stopped me.

"No, you have to try it! Trust me," he said with a wink.

I looked at the fruit, skeptical, but decided everything I was going to eat that night was going to be a new experience, so I cheered him again and took a big bite. I immediately understood why he made the face. It actually did taste like liquor, specifically rum. I didn't even actually get any fruit in my mouth. Just the juice. He laughed at me as I made a strange face. "What is that?" I asked as I adjusted to the taste in my mouth.

"It's called pickle fruit," Talents said as he took another bite, followed by a pained face. I laughed again at his silliness. "Don't eat too much of this. It will relax you if you have a little, but if you have too much, it will make you sick."

"How do you know what's too much?" I asked, a little concerned.

"Honestly, it's different for everyone. Just to be careful. I wouldn't eat any more of it. I just wanted to see your face." He patted my shoulder while he grinned at me. I didn't know Talents well, but he seemed like a good guy.

He stood up, and I reached out my hand to stop him. "Don't go," I pleaded. I had Tierly with me, but it was nice knowing someone else.

He took my hand and kissed it, which I wasn't expecting. He gave me a sympathetic smile. "I have to go, or someone," he said as he nodded his head down the table, "will get jealous. She's having a hard enough time right now with you getting all of Tierly's attention. Don't wanna make her too mad."

I realized he was talking about Sayrah, and I looked over to see her scowling in my direction. Talents looked at her too and rolled his eyes. "I'll see you soon."

I stopped looking at Sayrah because she made me very nervous. Instead, I looked at the table. Everyone was chatting and serving themselves the delicious-smelling food. I noticed my square plate in front of me already had some food on it. It looked like some sort of fish and grains filled with green and red vegetables. I glanced at Tierly, who was looking down. Her plate was empty. "Did you make this?" I asked her.

"Yes," she said as she lifted her head to look at me.

"But I don't remember you taking any food down," I said.

"Oh, yeah, there's a teleportation chamber in the kitchen area in our bungalow," she answered.

I stared at her closely. Something was wrong. She had a sadness in her eyes. "Why aren't you eating?" I asked even though I had many more questions. Tierly had never been one to eat very much, but I understood now that was because she normally only ate once a day.

"Oh…" she said with the same sullen smile. "Those crack noodles on the ship were enough for me. But you should eat."

I contemplated what she said. I was definitely hungry, but I was worried about her. I was haunted by her words that she was dying. Maybe her sadness had something to do with that. She turned away from me and stared down at the table; obviously, there was something on her mind. I thought about asking her, but I decided it wasn't the time for serious conversations. Everyone was smiling and laughing and enjoying themselves. So I decided I would too.

I looked beside my plate. There was something there that resembled a small clear spork. I wondered why everything they owned seemed to be made of glass. But I picked up the spork, scooped up some fish, and took a bite. Immediately, the pleasure receptors in my brain went off. It felt like someone had put drugs in my food. I didn't really know what heroin felt like, but I could guess that was it. I let out an audible moan as I remembered I had to chew my food.

Tierly looked at me and laughed. "That good, huh?"

I nodded my head slowly as I savored every taste and swallowed my first bite. For a moment, I was very content.

But before I had a chance to enjoy another bite, I heard the loudest, most terrifying scream come from the forest behind me. I turned quickly and looked frantically at the forest. Was that a person? I heard another scream, got up from my seat, and took a few steps toward the trees. I couldn't quite tell where it was coming from, but it was close. The person in trouble couldn't be that far away.

Tierly quickly grabbed my arm. "Don't do it," she ordered.

I turned to look at her and noticed not one person at the table was even paying attention. I wondered if they hadn't heard the loud cries. "But someone is in trouble!" I said desperately. "Didn't you hear the screams?" I started thinking about all the screams I had heard on Earth after the first attack. Fear and desperation exploded inside of me. I started to hyperventilate. Once again someone needed help, and Tierly wouldn't let me. I tried to jerk my arm away from her but was once again reminded of her strength as she held tight. I turned my attention back toward the forest as I heard another blood-curdling scream. That time, it was even closer, probably right at the edge of the forest. I could help them if Tierly would just let me go. "Please!" I begged. "I have to help them!"

"No!" Tierly said firmly. "It's not a person. It's a monster. It's trying to trick you. Trust me, no one needs help. It's a trap."

I looked back and forth between Tierly and the forest. My breathing was still erratic. I tried to process what she was saying, but I heard another scream. I tried again to pull away from Tierly, but she was too strong. I was still trying to tear away, but she pulled me closer. I hesitated, then I finally focused on what she had said: "It's not a person. It's a monster. No one needs help." I didn't relax at all, but I let her pull me away from the woods and back to the table. I heard another scream and looked desperately at Tierly and asked, "What is that?"

Tierly led me back to my seat. Everyone was still chatting, laughing, and eating. No one seemed to give one thought to the sounds coming from the forest except Quesa. She had a sad look in her eyes and was staring at her full plate. Why was she suddenly so unhappy?

I felt sick. I couldn't eat anymore. There was a glass full of clear liquid on the table. I picked it up with my shaking hands and took a few sips without asking what it was. The cool liquid tasted like water but with a little sugar added to it. I liked it, but I didn't enjoy it at that moment. I was too overwhelmed. About every ten seconds, I would hear a scream. Tierly closed her eyes, let out a sigh, and looked at me. "What you hear in the forest is what we call an Ancestor," she said.

"An ancestor?" I asked. What a strange thing to call a monster.

Before Tierly could explain, I felt a hand on my leg. I turned away from Tierly and looked down at the small hand. It was Quesa. How had she gotten next to me so fast? She still looked unhappy, but she grabbed my hand.

Tierly said, "Quesa, why don't you go sit down."

"No, Mother," Quesa said in her sweet, dejected-sounding voice.

I reminded myself to ask Tierly why they called her Mother. I couldn't imagine that all those people were her actual children. But then again, I had been surprised by almost everything that had happened in the last day or two, so that possibility probably shouldn't have been that strange to me.

"Knor," Quesa said, "would you like to see my real mother?"

Tierly chimed in. "Quesa, let's not overwhelm Knor on his first day here."

"No," I said. "I wanna see what Quesa wants to show me." I was already so overwhelmed that whatever she wanted to share couldn't make me feel much worse.

Tierly gave me a disapproving look, but I turned to Quesa, who continued to look despondent through her tiny smile. She grabbed my hand and led me to the very edge of the forest. I was nervous because we were literally right next to the trees. I could reach my arm out and pull leaves off if I wanted to.

Suddenly, the screaming was right in front of us. I tried to step back, but Quesa held my hand tight. Why were Links so strong?

"It's okay," she said. "There's a barrier over the forest. Nothing can come more than a foot beyond the trees. But the creatures don't like light, so they don't normally come out anyways."

That was when I saw it, the monster that they called an Ancestor. It stepped about an inch past the tree line. Its hair was long and matted with dirt. Its eyes were black and sunken in. It snarled at us, and drool dripped from its sharp teeth. I couldn't tell the color of its skin because it was covered with dirt. It stood there for a moment and stared at us. Then, its face contorted into an expression of extreme desperation, and it let out a blood-curdling scream that sharply pierced my ears. Before I could even react, it suddenly stopped screaming, contorting its face into a snarl, and lunged directly at me. I panicked and fell back into the sand as it ran into the invisible barrier. Quesa still held my hand. I sat there for a moment, my heart racing. Whatever it was, it was trying to kill me.

"Hello, Mother," Quesa said as her voice cracked.

I couldn't look at her because I was terrified of the monster, but I could tell she was crying.

"This..." she said with a sniff, "is my mother. Mother, this is Knor. He's a human. His planet was just destroyed. He lives here now. I just..." She let go of my hand and wiped her eyes. I looked at Quesa briefly and saw her tears. But they weren't like mine. They looked like liquid metal. But she whispered under her breath. "I just wanted you to meet him."

The monster, who I then knew as her mother, tried its hardest to get through the barrier, snarling and growling the whole time. But Quesa was never scared. I got myself together and stood up, standing right next to Quesa across from the desperate creature. I couldn't believe how brave the young girl was. I put my hands on her shoulders and tried to comfort her as we stared at the monster.

Just then, I saw smoke oozing off the skin of the creature. It let out another blood-curdling scream and disappeared back into the woods.

"It's the light," Tierly said from behind me. She was standing and looking at me. "The sunlight will kill them in seconds, but the firelight will burn their skin if they're in it too long."

Quesa looked up at me with tears still in her eyes, but she had a smile on her face. "She used to be the most beautiful Link," she said as she wiped her tears. "But now she's the most terrifying Ancestor. She will pass on soon though. There are about ten ancestors in the forest. But her eyes are sunken in deep. She doesn't have much longer till she finally dies for good."

Quesa wiped her frozen tears and gave me a sweet smile. She kissed my hand, a gesture I was beginning to get used to, and ran off down the beach to the water.

I looked and saw there were a few children down by the water, splashing around. Quesa got there quickly and jumped in, smiling and laughing with her friends as if nothing had happened.

Tierly was right beside me. I looked at her and she motioned for me to start walking next to the forest. "What…" I started. "Why did Quesa say that was her mother? What was that?"

"That was an Ancestor," Tierly said plainly as we walked slowly beside the forest while the torches lit up the beach. "When a Link dies… Well, they don't really die. They turn into monsters, like the one you saw. That was, in fact, Quesa's mother. She died about a year ago and now roams the forest. She'll be there for a few years, but eventually, she'll die from starvation, and then she'll no longer haunt this forest."

It took me a second to process what she was saying. We walked in silence while I pondered. Luckily, the screaming had stopped.

After a moment, I asked, "How do you know she'll die from starvation?"

"Because Ancestors survive off the blood of Links," she said. "And since they're trapped in the forest, they cannot feed. So it takes a while, but they'll eventually die."

"So… they're basically vampires?"

"Yes," she said plainly again. "When I finally die, that's what I will turn into."

I immediately stopped walking and stared at her in disbelief. I had almost forgotten she was dying. And then I was learning she would turn into a vampire. Or an Ancestor, as they called them. My eyes welled with tears, and a few fell down my cheeks. I didn't know what to say. I simply looked down and wiped my tears away.

"Don't worry," she said as she pulled me into her. We embraced in a much-needed hug. I continued to cry but felt comforted all the same. I wrapped my arms around her and took a few deep breaths. Tierly was dying.

I knew right then that I had to forgive her for lying to me about who she was. She'd said she had several years left, but I didn't want several years. I wanted my whole life with her. I leaned back, looked deep into her glowing green eyes, and kissed her.

Chapter Thirteen

The whole Ancestor event didn't bring me as much pleasure as I thought it would. I didn't realize it would be Quesa's real mother. As much as she got on my nerves, I didn't wish for her to be sad and I know seeing her mother in that state made her upset, even if she was a tough kid and didn't show it much.

I sat at the table for a while slowly picking at my food. I was discontent. A lot of things were on my mind. Mostly, what was I going to do when Mother died? I had Talents, but how would I handle seeing Mother in the forest at night, screaming that agonizing scream? I wasn't sure I could take it like Quesa did.

I looked around at the table. Most people had gone back up to their homes for the night. A few lingered drinking vine ales and talking. As I glanced at everyone, I got many smiles, but that was just the Link way; always kind. But I wondered how much these people cared for me? This brought another question, how much did I care for them? I was still very young for a Link. And if I have Mother's genes, I will live an exceptionally long life. But before I could think of anything else, Talents came over and smacked the back of my head.

"Ouch!" I said a little too loud. Everyone stopped their conversations to look at us.

Talents smiled and let out a fake laugh, "Just sibling stuff. No need to worry." He then grabbed my arm and pulled me away from the table.

"Hey! I wasn't done eating and why did you hit me? What did I do?" I stumbled as he pulled me closer to the shore.

"You know what you did," he said with a glare. "Did you see how sad you made Quesa and how scared Knor was? He almost jumped into the forest to save someone that would have murdered him in an instant.”

I jerked my arm out of his grasp. I did have a little more respect for Knor after seeing his courage on Earth and in Maltina. He did care about helping people, which was a very Link-like quality, and I admired him for it.

I thought about arguing with Talents, but I pursed my lips and simply asked with a tiny smile, “How did you know I instigated it?”

“I didn’t until right now,” he said with a wink.

I scowled, but quickly turned it to a small smile and smacked him on the arm.

***

The kiss was short and sweet. I would have kissed her longer, but Tierly pulled away. She gave me a smile and held my hand for a moment, but soon after, let go of it. She looked away and ran her fingers through her hair. I began to feel like maybe she hadn’t wanted me to kiss her. Maybe she was over us as a couple. I definitely wasn’t ready for anything serious again, but I had thought the kiss would have been fine.

We stood there in silence for what felt like an hour, but it was probably only a minute. I wasn’t sure what to say, and she just kept looking down. I decided to break the awkward silence by asking, “Why do they call you Mother?”

“It’s kind of an interesting reason,” she stated, finally looking at me again. “You see, most Links have a complicated start to life, as I think some have shown you.”

I recalled the memories that had been shared with me by some of the other Links. The images floated around in my head sporadically, but I did remember they all started out with Tierly taking them away from someplace else. And they were surrounded by strange species. I shivered as I remembered the monsters from my dream.

"You see," she started, "most Links are born from different species. For example, humans could have given birth to a Link. Links are special and unique. Unfortunately, this is what makes them so hated but also loved."

I looked at her with a confused look. How could a human give birth to a Link? And why were they both loved and hated?

"Links are a genetic mutation," she said. "I couldn't tell you why they're born or even how, I can just tell you what I know."

I thought about that for a moment. I had never heard of a human being born with purple skin. "You said most Links were born from different species and a human could even give birth to a Link. But has that actually happened?" I asked.

Tierly paused for a moment and looked at the ground, but eventually, she said, "I… don't think so. I have never known a Link to be born to a species as young as yours. Normally, it's millions of years into advanced evolution before Links show up among another species."

I felt a little disappointed by that statement. I thought humans were pretty far into evolution. It made me wonder how far along other species were compared to humans and how little I truly knew about the universe.

"Why do you take Links from their homes?" I asked. "Can't they just live with the species they're born to?"

"It's… complicated," she said. "You see, Links are either hated or worshipped by other species. And both are bad things. Hated obviously means they are often killed as soon as a purple-skinned baby is born. So we have to take them away in order for them to have a chance at life.

"But the worst thing is when Links are worshipped. You would think this would mean a life of happiness and luxury, being worshipped by the species they're born to. However, that's never the case. If they are worshipped, species do some of the craziest things. Like sacrificing them once they reach adulthood in cruel, barbaric ways. Or forcing them to exist as living gods with no freedoms or hopes for a normal life. One species that worships Links keeps them in a small room and drains them of all their blood every day knowing Links can survive the blood loss. But it causes them great pain to lose all their blood." She paused for a moment, closed her eyes, and took a deep breath. It looked like she was in agony as if she felt what the Links who were left to their original species would feel.

"But how do you know when a Link is born so you can save them?" I asked, hoping to distract her from her pain.

She lifted her head up and smiled. "I get a feeling," she said.

"A feeling?" I said aloud.

"Yes," she whispered. "I get a tingling feeling in my hands that rises up my arms. And into my mind comes the images of the new Link soon to be born. Then suddenly, I'm flying through the universe, and I can see what solar system and planet they'll be born in."

"But how?" I asked. "How do you see this? Does every Link see the same thing?"

"No," she answered. "I'm the only one who sees them being born. It was a gift that was passed onto me by another Link, by my mother, and I'll pass it on to another Link before I die. But that's why they call me Mother. I did not birth them, but I brought them here from their original life. I raised them all, so they all call me Mother."

"What about Talents and Sayrah?" I asked. She'd said they were her children, but I just learned that all of the Links considered her their mother.

Tierly laughed. "Yes, Talents and Sayrah are my real children. I actually birthed them." She smiled and looked in the direction of Talents and Sayrah. I saw love in her eyes. But it was the same love she had for all the people of Maltina. They really were all her children. It made me question again how old Tierly actually was.

"What about you?" I asked. "Were you born here, or were you saved by someone?"

Tierly stood there and gave me a despondent look. "I was born to a species called Scathyns," she said. "On my planet, Links were considered a curse from the gods. They would be taken from their home and slaughtered. My 'Mother' who saved me, gave me my powers. She is also gone now."

"How do you get your… powers?" I asked.

"Oh yes," Tierly started. "Before the 'Mother' Link dies, she breathes her powers into her protégée. Then the new Mother senses when Links are born and can rescue them if their species does not accept Links. Which is common."

"*Breathes her powers…*" I whispered to myself, although Tierly heard.

"Haha, I can't show you," she said. "I'm not dead yet! But you will see."

I wondered. "What happened to your real mother?" I asked.

"Oh, she died many, many years ago," she said sorrowfully. "Scathyns don't live very long. I only have a faint memory of her."

I looked around for a moment at everything around me and pondered what she had said. I wondered if it was a miserable life living as long as she had, seeing so many people she loved die. I felt like I would just be another person she outlived. But then I remembered she was dying, and I quickly became sad. I wished she would outlive me. I didn't want to be left on this planet without her.

As I stood there, my knees suddenly became weak. I was once again overwhelmingly tired. I let out a large yawn and looked at the people who were still chatting and eating. I remembered the screams from the forest, and that caused a shiver down my spine. I was glad that had stopped.

Tierly must have noticed my yawn because she said, "I think you may be done for the night."

I wobbled a little and let out another yawn. She was right. I was once again a cooked noodle. I felt like I had slept so much recently, and yet, I was still so tired.

Tierly asked, "Would you like anything else to eat before we go back up?"

I looked back at the long table. The food did look good, but I had lost my appetite, so I shook my head.

Tierly placed her hand on my shoulder and motioned for me to start walking. As we passed the table, almost everyone said, "Goodnight, Mother." Talents gave me a wink, while Sayrah gave me a scowl. I looked off at the shoreline. Six small children, including Quesa, splashed around in the firelight. It was weird to see such young-looking children with no one watching them. But after hearing how long everyone lived, I wondered if Quesa was older than me.

We made our way to the ladder, and Tierly said, "Remember, just think of where you wanna go," and she disappeared up the ladder. I decided to be as brave as possible. I only hesitated for about five seconds before I stepped next to the ladder, thought of Tierly, and was carried to the very top. I stepped off quickly and watched as Tierly jumped into the hole while I stumbled into the bungalow. I was nowhere near as graceful as Tierly.

I stood in the small room, staring at the four doors in front of me. I couldn't remember which one was the sleeping room. They all just said "Door controls" on the outside. I walked over to the door farthest to the left, which was the living room, thought real hard, and then I remembered my room was the farthest to the right. "Do you need anything?" she asked.

I thought about that for a moment, but the only thing I could think of was to ask her if she wanted to stay with me in my room. But after the way she handled our kiss, I decided not to push it. But I did have something else on my mind. "Why does Sayrah dislike me so much when all the other Links seem very welcoming and loving?"

Tierly took a step toward me. She paused and thought for a moment. She had a pained look on her face as if she was hurt by something. She exhaled and said, "Sayrah is an unusual Link. Most Links are selfless and can live in this utopia-type society, but Sayrah... she doesn't like to share. She doesn't really like anyone except Talents and me. She gets very jealous when someone else is getting my or Talents' attention. That's why she doesn't like you. But it has nothing to do with you. She dislikes everyone. Her birth was a difficult one. She was a breach baby and I was in labor a long time before she came out. I don't know if she didn't have enough oxygen and it messed with her mind. I noticed it when she was young and just thought she would grow out of it. But, unfortunately, she never did. I've tried to understand, but I've never been able to. Everyone just kind of accepts her, as any Link (except she), would, and let her be... grumpy all the time. She can be sweet to Talents and me, but you may never see that side of her.

"You see, if you and I hadn't found each other before the attack on your planet, there's no way I could have saved you. And that's what Sayrah wishes had happened. All the other Links consider it a blessing that you survived, but Sayrah... she just thinks differently. It worries me to consider what's going to happen to her mental state when I die." Tierly paused and closed her eyes. A few silver tears slipped out, and her bottom lip quivered a little. But she took a deep breath and wiped the tears from her eyes. She smiled at me with an unhappy smile. "I'm glad I saved you."

She pushed the button to the living room twice and disappeared inside. I thought about following her, but I didn't want to seem pushy. I just wanted to make sure she was okay. I hadn't seen her cry in a while. I couldn't decide if she was weeping because she was worried about Sayrah or if it had something to do with me.

I pushed the door control button to my room twice and made my way in. The large window in the room was less frightening. Somehow, being up so high had become exhilarating. I took a few hesitant steps toward the dim window. I didn't make it all the way, but I could see the sand and forest below me. All the people of Maltina were dancing on the beach. I couldn't hear the music, but they were all fluttering about, holding hands, and prancing around. A few people still sat at the table, but as I looked around, I didn't see anyone playing any instruments. Maybe they had some kind of stereo down there that I couldn't see. I also wondered what kind of music Links listened to. They were all jumping around, so it must have been upbeat. Suddenly jealous, I wished I had stayed down there to dance. But as I thought that, I let out a long yawn. Maybe I did need some sleep.

I looked around the room, and to my left, there was a symbol for bed. I put my hand on it and instinctively thought of my bed on Earth. Within seconds, a bed materialized beside me, and to my surprise, it was my bed! It was a king-size bed that even had my body pillow and the same red sheets I needed to wash. I put my hand on the bed slowly, feeling the soft fabric, the down comforter, and the pillows. It definitely felt like my bed. The only thing that was missing was Tierly.

I sat down on the edge of the plush bed and lay down without even getting under the covers. I rolled over, grabbed my body pillow, and fell deeply asleep.

Chapter Fourteen

I guess I had been affected by my behavior that night so I couldn't sleep. I thought about going into the hibernation tub and forcing myself to sleep, but I decided against it. Maybe it was good to stay up and ponder why I felt this way. It wasn't like me to feel guilty. Maybe if Talents hadn't guessed that I started the Ancestor screaming I wouldn't feel guilty. But I didn't like that thought because then I was caring about what people thought of me and I wasn't in the business of doing that.

So I laid in bed, staring up at the smooth black ceiling all night, wondering what names to put to these strange feelings.

It wasn't until maybe an hour after the sun had come up that I heard people stirring. I decided I was just going to be tired today. I kept wondering why I felt this guilt, but not even a night of pondering could come up with anything.

I changed clothes, which was just me putting on a clean gown. Links definitely weren't known for our style. A simple colored cloth gown was all we wore most of the time.

I walked out of my room and went into the common room where I heard Talents and Mother.

"Ah, you're awake," Mother said. "We are going to see the dragons today. Do you want to come? We are going to surprise Knor." She had a big grin on her face.

I gave her a blank look, but I did think about it. I haven't seen the dragons in a few years so it would be nice to visit them. "I would have liked to go alone…" I started but then sighed. "But I guess we can all go. I'll wake up Knor."

Both Talents and Mother gave me a suspicious look, but before they could say anything, I slipped into Knor's room.

***

As I slept, I dreamed again. This time, I was walking on the shore where the kids had been playing. I was wearing one of the cotton nightgowns it seemed everyone on Maltina wore. Feeling something in my hand, I looked down. I was holding the hand of a very light-purple-skinned person. As I looked beside me, I felt a rush of happiness when I realized it was Tierly. She was smiling at me lovingly. I grinned back at her.

I felt something on my legs and realized I was knee-deep in the water. It felt cool and warm at the same time. I touched the water with my free hand and looked up at the beautiful blue sky; there wasn't a cloud in sight. I could feel the warmth from the sun, but it wasn't too hot. It was just right.

I stopped walking and looked at Tierly. I put my wet fingers on her cheeks and watched a few drops trickle down. She was beautiful. I leaned into her welcoming lips and gave her a sweet kiss. Electricity rushed through me. I had never felt more loved than I felt right then.

Unfortunately, I was abruptly woken up by something hitting me in the face. I lifted my hands to defend myself and opened my eyes, trying to process my surroundings and what hit me. As I looked around, Sayrah was standing beside me with one of my pillows. She had a scowl on her face, and her eyes flashed with unhappiness. It wasn't a pleasant face to wake up to.

"Get up," she growled. "We're all going to see the dragons." She had an unamused look on her face. She threw the pillow at me, scoffed, and walked through the door. She reminded me of what it would have been like to have a sibling. I grew up as an only child, so I never experienced sibling rivalry. I wondered if that was what it felt like—both of us vying for Tierly's love. It was a strange feeling. I didn't like it. I also didn't like being woken up by a pillow attack to the face.

I was groggy, but I started to process what she had said. We were going to see the dragons? I questioned my memory, but I was almost certain that was what she had said. Since I had no context, I just let it slide. I looked around my room. Dim light shined through the large tinted window, and I could tell it was probably bright outside.

I tried to cling to the dream I was having, but as quickly as I had been woken up, it disappeared too. All I could remember was happiness, and I held on to that as I rolled out of bed. As soon as I stood up and got my footing, I turned around and noticed the bed had completely vanished. Before I had time to process it, Tierly was standing in the doorway.

"You ready to see something cool?" she asked with a huge grin on her face.

"Dragons?" I said hesitantly.

"Aw man," Tierly said, disappointed. "Did Sayrah tell you? It was supposed to be a surprise." She huffed. "I knew I shouldn't have let her wake you up, but she was too fast."

I became nervous after she confirmed I had heard Sayrah correctly. We were going to see dragons! My heart quickened its pace. I was overly excited and also terrified.

When people asked, I always said my favorite animal was a dragon, even at the age of twenty-seven. I had many small statues and drawings of dragons, as well as some books that talked about the different dragon lore in various cultures. And, apparently, we were about to go see some. I was wide awake then, so I skipped over to Tierly.

"Come on," she said as her smile returned.

I hopped out of the room, filled with energy, but unsure of what to say. A huge grin was plastered on my face. I had a lot of questions about the dragons, but the most important of all was whether we could ride them—assuming they could fly. I also wondered what they looked like and how big they were. However, I tried to remain calm. I didn't want to seem naive and childish. Although I couldn't contain my smile, I took a deep breath and was ready to follow directions. I imagined dragons were probably dangerous, and I needed to be calm and collected for the adventure.

Talents and Sayrah were in the hallway outside my room. Sayrah glared at me, then made her way out of the bungalow.

Talents looked at me and said, "Hello, Knor. How did you sleep?"

"Honestly, I don't even remember falling asleep, but I had a good dream, and now I feel refreshed. I could have been woken up more… gently," I said as I looked up in Sayrah's direction.

Talents laughed. "If it makes you feel any better, she woke me up the same way."

"Okay, everyone," Tierly said. "No more talking. Out of the bungalow. We've waited long enough for Knor to wake up." She looked at me with a playful grin and winked. "Time to see the dragons before they think we aren't coming and fly away for the day."

I gasped; they could fly. Also, how did someone make plans with a dragon? Tierly said they knew we were coming.

I basically jumped up the ladder to the top of the bungalow. Didn't want to keep the dragons waiting! Sayrah had disappeared. I stood with my back right up against the rock wall. I was getting used to being up so high, but I was still scared of falling. Tierly and Talents came up quickly behind me. Talents got on the lift and made his way down. Tierly motioned for me to also go down, and I leaped onto the lift, closed my eyes, thought of the sand below, and was transported down. As soon as my feet touched the sand, I opened my eyes and took a few steps forward toward Talents and Sayrah, who were waiting for us. I wondered why Sayrah even wanted to go. She didn't look happy.

I decided not to worry about Sayrah. I was going to have a good day despite her attitude.

I looked around the beach. There were a few people sitting on the sand while, once again, six children were playing on the shore. They seemed too young to be left alone so often. What if one of them drowned? But no one appeared to be worried about them.

Other people were going in and out of the forest. The ones coming back had small baskets filled with fruits and veggies, while one guy was leading a goat-like creature. It looked very old and was walking slowly. It stopped for a moment, and the man who was leading it bent down and picked it up. He carried the medium-sized creature with ease and made his way over to another lift farther down from us.

I asked, "Where are all these people coming and going from?"

Tierly appeared behind me and answered the question. "From the farms and livestock areas," she said. "They're just preparing for tonight's feast."

"Who tends the farms?" I asked.

"We all do," Tierly answered. "I told you last night. This is a utopian society. Everyone pitches in."

That statement probably should have made me feel good about Links, but it actually made me more cautious. Every book I had ever read that dealt with utopian societies always had a catch; it was never as perfect as people made it out to be. But, still, I nodded my head to affirm that I understood.

Tierly walked past me, and I followed as we made our way to the forest. I hesitated at the entrance that had just opened for us. What about the creature from last night? The one that was Quesa's mother. "What do we do about the vampires?" I asked. "Sorry, I mean the ancestors."

"Oh, it's fine during the day," Tierly said. "They hide underground when the sun is out. They dig holes in the ground. That's why they are so dirty. But there's nothing to worry about. Just the little bit of sun that seeps through the trees is enough to kill them. They are deep underground"

I looked at Tierly suspiciously, but she stepped into the forest behind Talents and Sayrah, so I followed. Once again, as we made our way through, the path in front of us opened up, leading us through the forest. I wondered if it was like the ladder, and I just had to think of where I wanted to go and the forest would lead the way. It was scary, though, because, behind us, the path we had just walked through was closing. I hoped if I ever got lost, the forest would save me by opening up the passageway to safety and not trap me inside with the monsters.

We made our way along the short path through the forest and ended up at the opening where the spaceships were. I wondered if we had to fly to where the dragons were, but instead, we continued on, weaving through the ships and into another forest on the other side. That one didn't open up like the other one, but there was a path leading through the woods. I stayed close to Tierly. The forest was darker and the trees more twisted. It made me nervous.

We made our way through the short path, and then I saw them: the dragons. Tierly, Talents, and Sayrah walked into the open field, but I stayed back at the edge of the woods. I trembled at the sight of them. They were around twenty feet from the ground up to their long necks. I couldn't tell how long their wingspan was because their wings were down, but I guessed they had to be at least forty feet. I saw three of them, and they were all covered in scales of different colors.

The one closest to me was an emerald color. I stepped back a little ways into the forest, but I couldn't take my eyes off of it. My jaw was wide open, and I hid behind a tree. Its teeth were bare, and it snarled at Tierly. I thought it was a sign of aggression and screamed at Tierly,

"Look out!"

But she simply walked over and caressed the beast. It kept baring its razor-sharp teeth, but that didn't faze Tierly. She whispered something to it, and it looked over at me. Its piercing eyes stared into my soul. I think quite literally.

And then I heard something. It was a faint whisper. But it was in my mind. It was as if someone was controlling my thoughts. The whisper said, "Hello, Knor. I am pleased to meet you. Come out from your hiding space, and let me see you. I promise—I don't bite people I like."

"Come on," Sayrah said impatiently. "Her name is Sabine, and she's a wonderful creature."

Sayrah started walking toward me, and she made me uneasy, so I stepped farther back into the forest. She let out a groan.

"Oh, come on!" she said, frustrated. "Grow a pair!"

I heard Talents let out a faint giggle, but Tierly was not amused. "Sayrah, be patient," Tierly said with very little patience for Sayrah in her own voice. "Knor, please come out. Sabine would like to meet you."

That was when I decided I needed to be brave. All three of them were standing beside the snarling, gigantic monster. So, surely, I'd be fine. Right?

I took a deep breath and stepped slowly out of my hiding space. I made it about an inch past the threshold of the forest before I froze. The dragon was still baring her teeth, but Tierly had her hand on the dragon's head. I looked at the sharp scales that were lying along its spine. Tierly smiled at me and motioned for me to come closer. I wanted to, but I couldn't make my legs go anywhere at that moment.

I looked at the massive creature whose name was apparently Sabine. Her skin was a luscious silky green with dinner-plate-sized scales covering her whole body. Her eyes were large and a glowing lavender color, much like Tierly's skin. She suddenly stood on all fours, her gigantic claws digging into the grassy ground. As she stood, her wings expanded. I almost fell over as the cool wind rushed past my face. I couldn't tell if the tears that came to my eyes were because of the wind or just how beautiful she was.

I heard a whisper in my mind. "Well, thank you."

"Can you hear her?" Tierly asked.

"Yes," I said in a whisper just like I had heard in my head. I had never seen anything more magical. Her expanded wings came back down beside her as another gust of wind rushed past me. This time, I laughed. "Wow…"

"Come to me," Sabine, the dragon, whispered in my mind.

I took a few steps and made it to her face. She was snarling still, but I began to realize since she wasn't a dog, a snarl must mean something different to her. She then stretched her neck out and nudged me with her head. I reached my hand out and touched her. I couldn't believe it. I was touching a dragon! I petted her rough scales, amazed by her beauty. I looked at Tierly with misty eyes. There were so many emotions I wanted to express. I was happy I was petting a dragon, but I was sad I didn't get to share this experience with my deceased friends and family. They were gone and would never experience the incredible things I was experiencing.

I shook my head to get back to reality which was more unreal than anything I had experienced. But I did wonder, "How did the dragons get here?" I asked as I smiled and stroked Sabine.

"They came with us," Tierly answered. "Dragons normally live on planets, but they can fly through space. They escaped the last attack on Links and came here with us. And they are much older than Links. I've known Sabine since I was a child."

I pondered the notion of dragons flying through space. I wished they had lived on Earth. But then I looked at Tierly. I smiled. She had saved me from destruction and was now sharing her life with me. It struck me how much I really cared about Tierly. She was my last connection to my planet and life there. I had to know her, whole mind, body, and soul. And I could only think of one way to do that. One way to truly know her and trust her. I looked at her and asked, "Could you share your core memories with me the way some of the other Links did?"

Tierly took her hand off Sabine, and she looked seriously at me. Talents and Sayrah had wandered a few feet away, but they heard the question and turned around.

"No," Sayrah said. "Those memories aren't for you to see."

"Sayrah," Tierly said.

"No!" Sayrah said forcefully. "It'll take all of her energy to share her memories with you. It's different for her. She's older. Her memories are more intense. It'll make her weak for hours."

"Stop being dramatic," Tierly said. "Knor, I'll show you my memories. I can get in the immersion tub afterward and be back to normal in a minute. But I will warn you, it's not the same as the other Links. It's not just a small flash of images. It's immersive. Are you sure you wanna see?"

Sayrah literally growled and then stomped away.

I looked at Tierly and said, "Yes."

Tierly took her hand off Sabine and stepped next to me. She shook her hands and took a deep breath. "You ready?" she asked with a grin on her face.

I nodded, but I wasn't prepared for what happened next.

Chapter Fifteen

It felt wrong for Mother to share her memories with Knor. It was the last thing that was just a family thing and now he would know her whole past. Mother hadn't even shared her memories with anyone else on Maltina. Just Talents and me. And in her state with her heart no longer beating, this would take so much energy from her.

And also I had a feeling. I don't know why, but it just seemed like a bad idea. Like we would need Mother's energy for something else. Why couldn't they just ride dragons and call it a day?

I did have another naughty thought. Knor was a human and their brains aren't super advanced. I wondered if maybe the shock of seeing her memories would kill him. It was a very bad thought, but I couldn't help it.

Unfortunately, it didn't kill him. But it did turn out we would need Mother's powers soon.

***

The ground below me opened up and, suddenly, I was falling. I thrashed about in the air and screamed. I knew I was about to die. I must have been standing in a sinkhole. I managed to survive my planet being destroyed, but I was going to die in a sinkhole.

As I fell, I realized there was no wind rushing around me, and there weren't any rocks or debris falling beside me. I looked around and discovered I wasn't falling. I was floating in darkness. There was no beginning or end to it, just darkness as I floated. I was terrified. How would I escape? Was I trapped there forever? What had happened?

Around me, I unexpectedly felt warmth. I heard whispers. A

strange alien woman was holding me. And I was no longer myself. I was suspended in the air staring at myself, except I was no longer me. I was a dark-purple-skinned baby. I had just been born.

The woman holding me had long tentacles dangling down her head, and she was crying. I could hear her beg. "Please," the woman said. "This can't be happening. This is my baby."

Another very light-skinned purple woman stood before the crying tentacle lady and kept saying, "You know what they'll do with her. I have to take her with me. Please, give me the baby."

The woman holding me just started sobbing, holding on even tighter to me. I knew she was my mother. "But she's my baby!" she cried. "I… I'll leave this planet and take her with me. We can hide. Or you can take me with you. I'll go with you." She pleaded desperately with the woman.

"I can't take you," the purple woman said. "You know that. Your species and my species have an agreement. You can't live with us. Just the Links born to you can come."

"We won't tell them!" she begged. "Please, don't take my baby!" Her crying continued. But it was all for naught. The purple woman said, "I'm sorry," and lifted me from my mother's arms. She continued to sob, but the beautiful woman took me anyway.

After being taken away, I was myself again, floating in a black abyss. I struggled to see around me, but all I saw was darkness until I felt water. I was on a planet much like Maltina but not exactly the same. The light was more orange, and there were two suns! I felt the warmth from the sun mixed with the cool water I was splashing in. I was older, probably around Quesa's age. There were no other children with me, but the woman who had taken me from my mother stood by me, laughing as I played. And I knew her as my mother. I remember being a baby and being taken away from my true mother. But I knew the purple woman was also my mother, and I had so much love for her.

Again, the darkness came, and I floated aimlessly until I was surrounded by many Links. They were all holding hands around me in the candlelight. I was lying on the cool ground, and the woman I called Mother stood over me.

"I give you my gift," she said as she placed her hands over my heart and her open lips hovered above mine. She took a deep breath and exhaled into my soul. Suddenly, I was in immense pain. It was like she had stabbed my heart with a dagger. I winced and shook in agony. But then the pain was gone, and I could feel every Link around me. I sensed their life and experienced what they were going through. I was overwhelmed with emotion and felt love like I had never felt it before. I could see the future. I could see when another Link was about to be born even though it was years before it was actually going to happen. I could see it!

The darkness surrounded me again, but I wasn't scared anymore. I didn't feel content, but I was ready for the next memory. When it came, it was different—it was sad. I was older, maybe a young adult. I was standing at the edge of a pine forest, staring at the woman I had called mother. She screamed that same horrible scream I had heard before. And I was so unhappy. I cried and begged my mother to remember me. Instead, the woman reached her arm out into the candlelight and clawed at my arm, leaving a deep bleeding cut.

Even though I was plunged into darkness, my eyes quickly adjusted, and I looked at my arm. There was no cut or scar. Just smooth skin that had abruptly turned light purple. I looked at myself, and what I saw was odd and unexpected; I was pregnant. Twins, I knew. A boy and a girl. Something was wrong with the girl. I was told to give her away, but I couldn't do that. I was meant to be her mother. Links so rarely had children, and I was about to have two. I would raise them on my planet, which I called Maltina, but it was not the same planet I was living on with Tierly. I knew because it still had two suns.

Without drifting again into darkness, I ran as fast as I could while I was in labor. Fear filled every molecule in my body. I was scared for myself, for my unborn children, and for all my children whom I had saved during my long life. I looked up at the sky, and I saw the same gridded pattern I had seen on Earth. The orange light shone from the bottom of all the metal-rigged ships in the sky. Confusion engulfed me as I saw the memories of myself, Knor, and the memories of who I had become, Tierly. I knew it was the Zyeens. They had come for the Links as well.

I got to a Link spaceship as fast as I could. About half the Links were able to make it to a ship to put up a forcefield before the Zyeens attacked. And once they did, the planet was completely destroyed. We all put our ships into stealth mode and disappeared off what was left of the planet. I could sense that all the Links who didn't make it on the ships died. I felt their fear and their temporary suffering. But I also felt my pain. I was in labor, and I had to fly the ship. A few Links were with me on the ship, all scared for their lives and mourning the loss of loved ones. But I had two children that were ripping through me to get out.

I lay on the floor in the control room, and Talents was the first to come out. I held him close to me, and he didn't cry. He just had a big smile as he looked around the room. Next came Sayrah, who was difficult even at birth. It took awhile and she was breached, but she cried and thrashed about as she entered the universe. But the love I felt for them was strong. I loved all my children, but those two I loved so deeply that I couldn't explain it. I would have done anything for them.

The darkness enveloped me again. I felt pain in my stomach from giving birth, but it slowly faded away. Many years passed. I had a faded recollection of when they found Venus and colonized it as the new Maltina. Small memories of saving baby Links popped up. But nothing major happened until I saw myself, Knor.

I was on Earth, taking some time alone while Talents and Sayrah traveled the globe. As I looked at myself as Tierly, my heart fluttered. Tierly and I were sitting outside the drama room. I didn't even think she'd noticed me that day, but she had. She was torn, just like I was. She didn't know if she should talk to me or not. Before she even spoke to me, she already loved me so much. I wanted to get out of that darkness to tell her I felt the same way. That I had always loved her too.

But the happiness was short-lived. I came out of the trance Tierly had put me under to share her memories. I fell backward toward the ground but was caught by Talents. Tierly fell face-first, but Sayrah caught her. What I saw when I looked up at the sky sent shivers down my spine. I asked, "Am I still in a memory?"

Talents laughed. "No, you're here with us."

"Then what is that?" I asked, my voice trembling. Above me, floating suspiciously in the sky, were the square metal spaceships that had destroyed Earth. More and more appeared and created that terrifying grid-like structure.

Sayrah and Talents looked up and gasped.

"Fuck!" Sayrah shouted. "Mother, wake up! We need your forcefield now!"

Tierly blinked groggily and turned around to look up at the sky. Her eyes widened, but she struggled to get up.

"I can't," Tierly said desperately. She could barely stand. "We have to get to the ship."

Sayrah helped Tierly up and screamed at her, "What do you mean 'get to the ship?' What is everyone else going to do?"

Tierly tried to stand up on her own, but she fell over. "I can't," she said again, liquid metal tears streaming down her cheeks. "We have to get to a ship now. That's the only way we can put up a forcefield and survive the first wave. The other Links will know what to do. Please, help me! We have to run!"

Sayrah growled but lifted Tierly up on her shoulder. "Come on!" she screamed at Talents and me. Talents helped me to my feet and let me lean on him as we ran back through the second forest. I looked behind me as we were leaving the open field. I wondered what the dragons would do. Sabine whispered one last request to me, "Take care of them for me." And suddenly, all three dragons magically disappeared. I hoped they were going somewhere safe.

The ships weren't far, and when we got to them, many Links were already boarding ships since this had happened before. They all rushed in with no belongings or anything. I wondered if everything they owned would be lost.

I looked up again as the metal square ships started opening at the base. The wind rushed around us just like it did on Earth. That really woke me up as we made it to their ship, the ramp appeared, and we climbed up inside. Sayrah and Talents threw Tierly and me down onto the ground, and Talents closed the entrance to the ship and went to sit at the control panel. Talents said, "Shields are up." Then the orange light appeared, and everything outside the window was set on fire.

I continued lying on the floor of the ship as the orange fire engulfed everything around us. I didn't close my eyes as I had on Earth when we were hiding in Tierly's bubble forcefield. I kept my gaze on the large window that took up half the control room. A hurricane of fire engulfed the planet.

After several seconds of fire, the orange light disappeared, and the only thing I saw out the window was smoke. I grabbed my throat as I remembered the pain I had felt on Earth when I choked on the dirty air.

Slowly, the smoke began to clear, and I saw the destroyed land. The forest was in ruin, but I saw no other ships. "Where is everyone?" I asked.

"The ships are cloaked," Talents said as he stared intently at the glass panel.

Then the ten ancestors that lived in the forest came up out of the ground. The sun was now mostly shielded. They began running around, letting out their blood-curdling screams. I thought of Quesa, and tears came to my eyes. I saw the one that was her mother, covered in matted dirt and screaming as she ran. I imagined what it must be like for Quesa as she saw this. And then I wondered something sad: did she make it to a ship?

But before I could ask, there was a bright green flash and the ten ancestors were gone. I sat confused and suddenly even more scared. What if they came on the ship? "Where did the ancestors go?" I ask frantically.

"They took them to burn and give to their queen," Talents said with a whispered frozen voice.

I stood up hesitantly and stumbled closer to the window. The forest to our left was all embers and smoke. The once-sturdy bungalows dangled off the cliff, destroyed.

Everyone on the ship stared out the window. Tierly was still on the ground, but her face showed all of her emotion. Tears traveled down her cheeks. "No…" she whispered as her voice cracked.

Talents sat at the control panel with his hand over his mouth. He was slowly shaking his head. Talents slammed his hand down on the control panel and an electric shock ran through the ship. "Fuck!" he screamed. Sayrah stood beside Talents, using his chair to hold herself up, her face torn with anger and shock.

I focused my attention on Tierly. After a brief look of shock crossed her face, she quickly wiped her tears and looked at Talents.

"Do you have the cloak on?" Tierly asked Talents.

"Yes," he answered plainly, the word muffled as his hand was still over his mouth.

"We have to get off this planet," Tierly said while she rolled onto her knees and tried to stand up. "They're going to initiate phase two soon. We need to go before they start mining."

I stood right against the window and looked around. I stared at the sky and didn't see anything. Why were they leaving? I remembered Tierly telling me the Zyeens destroyed planets to get the metals to build more ships, and they attacked Links to get their powers. So why would they annihilate Maltina and then leave?

"Most of them are fine," Tierly said in a sad tone. "I can feel most of their life forces." She paused for a moment.

"There are twenty ships that are showing several life forms," Talents said.

"Send a message to the ships," Tierly said with almost no energy. "Tell them to meet us at Pluto."

We all stayed in our positions for a moment while we processed.

"Talents," Tierly stated. "I know what you are thinking."

"No," he said sternly. "It's my fault. There was a glitch in the forcefield around Maltina when we came back from Earth. I ignored it. I… I didn't think they would be able to track us back to the planet once we had the cloak over the ship. But I guess maybe when we came through the forcefield returning from Earth, the glitch must have allowed them to track us back to Maltina. I'm… I'm so sorry," he said as he put his face in his hands and started to sob.

Sayrah and I looked at each other at the same time. She just scoffed and walked to the other side of the control room and stood there with her arms crossed. I could tell she was holding back tears. She may have been mostly attached to Talents and Tierly, but I knew she probably cared for the other Links on Maltina too, and it was her home.

Tierly was suddenly standing behind me, and I jumped when she spoke. "We need to go," she said with a scratchy voice.

I could tell she still didn't have much energy from showing me her memories, but she was trying to be strong. I quickly got up from my spot on the floor. I walked over to Talents, who was still crying, and placed my hand on his shoulder. He leaned his head onto my hand and started taking deep breaths.

"We have to do it," Sayrah said from the other side of the room. She kept her glare through the window at the scorched ground.

"No!" Tierly said forcefully. "It's not our job."

"But it is our problem!" Sayrah said in defiance. "They've destroyed two of our planets. When are we going to stop being their punching bag?"

"We can't do it," Tierly said. "We took an oath that we would never use our powers to destroy. Only to save."

"So we're just going to let them get away with this again and again?" Sayrah shouted. "Maybe most species don't like Links, but they aren't actively trying to wipe out every single one of us. They destroyed this last Maltina, and we hid as best we could. But now… Links are dead! Again! But you didn't save them. You said when you rescued them all when they were born that you would always protect them. But now look! Our planet is destroyed. This was simply malice. They didn't even farm the planet. They destroyed it just to destroy us. We'll never be safe till the Zyeens are gone. No planet in any galaxy is safe. Fuck the oath."

I looked at Tierly, who had her head resting in her hand. I asked, "What oath?"

She didn't look amused by my question, but she answered it anyway. "Link technology is advanced," she started. "Far more advanced than most species. But there is a… council that many nearby species are a part of. Most species live in peace because of this council. It's made up of about one hundred different species within this Universe. Each has three representatives of its species. Links actually started this council, although we're not a part of it. However, we all took an oath that we would never take sides or influence any other species' planet with our technology or even simply our opinions. The only thing we're allowed to do is take baby Links from different planets and raise them as our own. But other than that, we keep to ourselves. Sayrah wants to break that oath by completely wiping out the Zyeens. To do this, we'd have to find the queen and kill her. She controls the Zyeens because, like I was telling you before, they're a hive species."

"Can you do that?" I asked.

"Do what?" Tierly asked.

"Find the queen and kill her?"

"Yes," Tierly answered plainly. "But we aren't going to," She said as sternly as she could in her weakened state looking directly at Sayrah.

"I'm with Sayrah," Talents said as he wiped his dried tears away. "This needs to stop."

"We would become the enemy of the council," Tierly pleaded as best she could.

"So what?" Sayrah said.

"Yeah," Talents chimed in. "We are stronger than the council. I think they would understand."

"And if they don't?" Tierly asked.

"Then we will fight them all!" Sayrah shouted. "We are stronger than any of those species."

"What if they break our truce and don't let us save baby Links?" Tierly asked. " Are you willing to take that risk?"

"Mother," Talents started, "we can still save baby Links. You know where they are. We can sneak onto planets to rescue them. We don't need to be part of the council."

"We have literally followed this path and all it has led to is our destruction," Talents stated. "We have to do something!"

Tierly sighed. I think she was too tired and weak for this conversation.

Sayrah turned to me unexpectedly and said, "We've literally run out of options, so, unfortunately, you are the only one left to weigh in on this. What do you think we should do, hitchhiker?"

I was taken aback by the question. But I thought about it. My opinion did matter, apparently. In a matter of a few days, I had lost my planet twice. So really, it was a no-brainer. "How long will it take to find the queen?" I asked.

"Not long," Talents answered.

"Then let's do it," I said with excitement in my voice. "If you can kill them, then I say we should. They've destroyed enough planets and lives. Fuck the oath. I'd love some revenge."

Chapter Sixteen

Sayrah looked at me with surprise and then grinned. I wasn't sure why, but I was filled with excitement, even though I had no idea what to expect. And I supposed I shouldn't have been excited about destroying a whole species. But from my small experience with them, the Zyeens deserved it.

"So what do we do next?" I asked, eyeing Tierly, who did not seem well. She swayed back and forth, her eyes slowly blinking. "Hey, are you okay?"

As soon as I asked, she fell to the floor. I leaped over to her to try and catch her, but she'd fallen too suddenly. Sayrah and I were both at her side. I lifted Tierly's head up and rested it on my lap. Her eyes kept opening and closing slowly. That was it. She was dying. Soon, she would be a monster like Quesa's mother. I'd lost everyone I loved. But Sayrah knew what to do and acted quickly.

"We need to get her in the immersion tub," she said as she lifted Tierly off the ground. I remember waking up in one of those when I was first brought to this ship.

"Is she dying?" I asked in a panicked tone.

"She's just exhausted," Sayrah said reassuringly. "She just needs to rest."

I let out a sigh of relief.

"Stay here with Talents. I'll take care of Mother." Before I could argue, Sayrah had whisked Tierly off down the passageway.

I looked at Talents. "How long will it take for her to recover?" I asked.

Talents was busy messing with the control panel, not listening to me. He seemed very focused. No longer crying, just concentrated on his new task: find the queen.

I started to think about all the people in Maltina living the perfect utopian life. Never bothering anyone. Just loving each other and spending time together. I thought of the Links who had been kind enough to show me their memories and how that was all they had become. Just memories. Where would we live? The excitement was vanishing. I was frightened. I felt comfortable in Maltina because all the people lived in harmony. But where would we go next? To a planet with nothing or to a planet with another species and try to cohabitate? How long had the Links wandered before they colonized Venus?

Before I could spiral too much, Talents answered the question I thought he hadn't heard. "She'll be fine in just a few minutes," he said.

I felt only slightly relieved. I still didn't know where we were going to live, how we were going to find the queen, or if we would even survive the next few minutes.

"Are the other Links going to follow us?" I asked.

"No," Talents answered, but he was still focused.

"Where will they go?"

Talents sighed. He obviously didn't want to talk right now. "They are going to hide around Pluto. I already sent out a message. They are cloaked and should be fine. But we need to find the queen.

"There," Talents said suddenly as he leaned back in his chair. I looked at the water control panel. There was a red spot on it. He smiled and said plainly, "Found you, bitch." He leaned forward toward the panel, and suddenly, the ship started rising. The motion made me wobble a little, but I didn't fall down.

"Just so you know, we may not make it through this," Talents said with a serious look on his face.

"What do you mean?" I asked.

"Well, this could possibly be a suicide mission. We're going to have to board the ship, make it past all the guards, and hope they don't catch us. Once the queen is dead, all her little minions will become useless. So we just have to successfully kill the queen without being killed ourselves."

I stood there for a moment staring at Talents. I guess I hadn't really thought about that. All I had considered was getting revenge. I hadn't considered the fact that the mission was a dangerous one. Was I really willing to die for revenge? But then it hit me. I had nothing but my life left to lose. Earth was gone; Maltina was destroyed. All I had left in the whole universe was on the ship.

The thought brought me back to reality, and it made me less fearful. All I had left to lose was my life. But everyone else in the universe was at risk while the Zyeens were still alive. What did my small life matter in relation to all the lives in the universe? My life just didn't seem as important anymore. I wasn't scared of losing it.

A smile crawled across my face. Talents looked at me with a concerned expression for a moment, but then he returned the smile. "All right then," Talents said as he returned his attention to the control panel.

Before I could say anything else, I heard Tierly from behind me, "How close are we?" she asked Talents.

"In two minutes, we'll be by their mother ship," Talents said from his post.

I looked longingly at Tierly, and she actually returned my glance with a smile.

"Are you better now?" I asked.

"Yes," Tierly said as she walked over to me and put her hand on my shoulder.

"So... what do we do once we get to the ship?" I asked.

Tierly laughed. "Well, you'll stay here with Talents," she said.

"What?!" Talents and I said at the same time.

"Talents needs to stay behind to control the ship, and you"—Tierly pointed at me—"are a liability. You don't know anything about spaceships or Zyeens or even our technology. I can't do what I need to do while I'm also looking out for you."

"I mean," Talents said, "I thought it was a suicide mission, and we were all going to go together. But, whatever, I guess I'll stay behind and guard the ship."

Tierly walked over to Talents and gave him a kiss on the forehead, which made him smile, and it seemed to lift his spirits. I, however, was still not amused.

"Please, Tierly," I asked. "I really want to help. I'm sure there's something I can do."

"No," Tierly said, looking at me. "I'm sorry, Knor, but it's too dangerous for you."

"But... how will I know you're okay?"

"Ah," Talents interjected. "I can help with that. Tierly, put on your glasses."

Tierly touched a small spot at the bottom of her ear where a small silver studded earring lay and those blue-tinted glasses appeared on her face. Then Talents pushed a few spots on the control panel. Suddenly, the large window became a screen, and I was on it because Tierly was looking at me.

"Now you can see everything she sees," Talents said. There was an echo in the room, and he added, "And hear."

I heard a faint beep and looked at the control panel. There was a small red dot on it. Talents were suddenly very serious. "We're here," he said.

I looked desperately at Tierly. "How are you going to do this?" I asked, unsure what the plan was. I knew she was going to kill the queen, but I wasn't sure how.

"Sayrah and I are going to disguise ourselves as Zyeens," she said as she lifted her arm up to show me her silver bracelet. She pushed what seemed to be an innocuous part of the bracelet, but in an instant, she was in the same Zyeens soldier garb that I had seen on Earth. It even made her a whole foot taller! Tierly pushed a button on the side of her sleek black helmet, and a small opening appeared where her face was. She still had her glasses on. "We're going to teleport down to the mother ship and kill the queen. We won't have much time because the queen will probably sense intruders, but we're going to teleport close to her lair on the ship."

"How close are we to the mother ship?" I asked.

"Talents, take the feed down," Tierly said.

Talents waved his hands methodically over the control panel, and immediately, right in front of us, was a large star-like ship. I panicked. There was no way we were that close. Surely the Zyeens could see us. We were right in front of their ship! I stepped back from the window and gasped, but Tierly placed her hand on my shoulder. "We're cloaked," she said as if that explained it all. "They can't see us."

I looked at her suspiciously. Everything was starting to worry me. "Are you sure this is a good idea?" I asked as I looked back at the large star-shaped ship.

"It's not a good idea," I heard from behind me. It was Sayrah. She also had on Zyeens soldier garb with her face showing, also sporting those same glasses Tierly had on. "But what are you gonna do? Gotta protect the universe. I'll be in the teleportation bay." Sayrah walked back into the passageway.

I looked back at Tierly. I grabbed her hand instinctually, wanting so badly to go with her. "Please… let me come with you. I can't lose you too," I said desperately.

She placed her hand on mine and smiled. "I'll be back soon," she said with lots of hope in her eyes. I smiled, but as I went to pull my hand away to let her leave, she held on tight. "Save this for me," she whispered as she leaned down and kissed me. It wasn't a long kiss or even a passionate one, but as she pulled away, it made me long for more. We had been through so much in the past few days, such as losing my home twice. I had thought many times we would never be together again. But as the past few days went on, this little drop of hope kept showing up. I wondered if maybe we could make it work. And this kiss, although rushed, showed me that she also still had hope. But then she turned and disappeared through the passageway.

I looked back toward the window. Talents had put up the feed from Tierly's glasses again. She was standing in the teleportation bay but only for a moment. Then it went black for a second before the feed picked back up, and she was in a large unfamiliar room. I realized they must have landed inside the ship. Tierly looked around the room, which was filled with what resembled cocoons. They were opaque, so I couldn't see what was inside, but I assumed that was how Zyeens were born.

Tierly looked around the room. Both she and Sayrah had those large guns I had seen the Zyeens carrying when they attacked Earth. I didn't remember seeing them with guns before they left. Maybe their multifunctional glass tablets could also turn into any type of weapon.

Tierly and Sayrah started to walk around the rows of cocoons in the doorless room. The cocoons slightly pulsated as if whatever was inside was breathing. I kept expecting a large spider to appear. And strangely enough, that was basically what happened.

Tierly and Sayrah walked through the dimly light den of cocoons until we heard a low growl. They both stopped and so did my heart.

Out of nowhere, crawling on the wall over some cocoons, a large creature appeared.

"That's a male Zyeens," Talents said as he stared at the screen. "Sayrah and Tierly are disguised as the unisex soldiers. There are only a handful of males."

The beast was probably eight feet tall with six legs and spikes for feet. It was a dark-brown color large thorns coming out from all over its head and long body. Its razor-sharp teeth snarled at Tierly and Sayrah. The creature went over to them slowly as if it wasn't sure what they were—as though it knew they looked like Zyeens but could tell something was off.

It walked with its six legs over to Tierly and Sayrah. They both stood their ground and had their guns at the ready. Before they could fire at the creature in front of them, Sayrah shouted, "Behind you!"

Tierly turned around, and the screen went dark.

My heart dropped. "What happened?" I demanded.

Talents was silent.

"Talents!" I screamed.

"The feed cut off," he said in a whisper as he messed with the control panel. He seemed calm, but his hands were shaking. "The Zyeens must have figured out they weren't one of them."

That was it. I was tired of sitting around, so I ran to the teleportation bay. I wasn't 100 percent sure how to use it, but I assumed it was like everything else the Links had built; I just had to think of where I wanted to go, and it would take me there.

"Wait!" Talents yelled before I made it to the passageway. "Take this." He handed me his little shiny black rock that turned into a tablet, a gun, and who knew what else.

"I have one," I said as I reached into my pocket and pulled it out.

"Just think of a gun, and it'll appear," he said as he stepped toward me and aggressively put his hands on my shoulders. "They're going to take them to the queen. They'll feed them to her. Here!" he said anxiously as he took his hands off my shoulders and handed me his silver earring. "This will show you the way once you get to the ship. Just push it," he said, stuttering from adrenaline.

I looked at the earring. It was just a gold metal circle. It didn't have any kind of back. I hesitantly put it up to my ear, and it stuck. "Thanks," I said as I turned away from him, and the glasses computer screen Tierly had on Earth appeared over my eyes.

"Good luck," he said with a sad look on his face. He didn't seem optimistic, but I had to try.

I went to the teleporter, stood under one of the glowing lights, and thought about Tierly.

Chapter Seventeen

I saw the second giant male Zeenan coming for Mother. I shouted to her, but it was too late. He was too fast. He reached his six large claw-like arms up and hit Mother so hard her cloak disappeared and she hit the ground hard in her normal clothes. Her pendant disappeared to another part of the ship and she lay unconscious in the ground. I collapsed on the slick ground beside her. She had a gash on her head and a little red-blue drifted out over her lavender skin.

I looked around. There were now three males around us. "Give me your device," one said in a raspy deep voice. Another one had already picked up Mothers. I scowled but handed him my pendant. I still had a few tricks, but I was waiting for the right moment to use them. "You can't hide from us anymore. Our technology has caught up with you, Link. We know your other ships are around the planet, Pluto. We will be there soon. We also know you have a ship 'cloaked' around this one. They will be destroyed soon. And you all will be coming with us."

Suddenly, there was a familiar swoosh sound and a bright light. The male Zeenan above us fell over and I looked over at the direction it came from. I was surprised, but whispered in a satisfied voice, "Hitchhiker."

***

I didn't think of Tierly exactly. Instead, I thought of the corner of the room she was in because I didn't want the Zyeens to see me when I appeared. I stood under the circle of lights and suddenly felt a rush of cold air around me. I closed my eyes out of fear but thought vehemently about the small spot in the room I had seen.

The cold rush of air disappeared, and I opened my eyes. I was surrounded by breathing slimy cocoons. In front of me were the ridged backs of three male spider-like Zyeens, while Sayrah and Tierly were on the moist ground. I stepped away quietly as I tried to not be seen, but as I leaned back, I felt stickiness all over me. I covered my mouth so I wouldn't make a sound in disgust when an unexpected rotten smell hit me.

Tierly was passed out, and Sayrah was sitting on her knees beside her. Both of them were out of disguise and in their regular cotton gowns. One of the Zyeens stood over Tierly and Sayrah, who still had their glasses on, but I wondered what had happened to their guns. Then I saw one of the other male creatures off to the side holding two black rocks in his hand.

I knew what I had to do. I held the small black rock and thought of a gun. The rock quickly shifted into a gun-like apparatus, and I aimed it at the monster that was standing over Tierly and Sayrah. I pulled the trigger twice. There was a faint "swish" sound and a pop of light, but other than that, it was basically silent. The Zyeens standing over them fell to the ground. I didn't think he was dead, just wounded. The other two male beings took their attention off of Tierly and Sayrah. I froze. I wasn't really sure what to do. But as they started raising their guns toward me, Sayrah took advantage of their distracted attention and screamed, "Close your eyes!" So I did, but right before I shut them, I saw the beginning of a bright flash similar to what she had created on Earth to escape the soldiers.

I heard a loud growl from the two monsters, but suddenly, I felt a hand on my shoulder. "Come on!" Sayrah ordered. I didn't open my eyes, but I let her hold my arm and drag me through the walls of cocoons.

"What about Tierly?" I asked in a panic as I opened my eyes. But I was relieved when I saw her draped over Sayrah's shoulder. I looked back at the Zyeens. They all were holding their spiked hands over their eyes. Sayrah's light must have hurt them. Then I looked at Sayrah.

She had a gun in her hand and was holding Tierly on her shoulder.

"How did you get your gun back?" I asked.

"I stole them quickly while they were blinded by my light," she said with a wink.

It amazed me how strong Links were. None of them had bulky muscles, but that was the second time I'd seen Sayrah carry Tierly like it was nothing.

We made our way to the end of the surprisingly large cocoon room where there was one small circle that didn't have any cocoons, although it was dripping with slime. Sayrah stopped and turned her gun into a glass tablet. "What the fuck," she said in an annoyed tone. "Where is she?"

All of a sudden, I felt something touch my shoulder. I looked and there was a strange red goo on me. I didn't touch it, but I asked Sayrah, "What is that?"

Sayrah stopped looking at her tablet and quickly looked at my arm. She gasped and looked up. "It's the queen!" she shouted as she stared at the ceiling. I looked up quickly and saw an even larger version of the male Zyeens crawling on the ceiling. She was vermilion, had eight legs and a large belly, and spikes covered her body. She snarled at me with her many sharp teeth, red spit dripping from her mouth.

The queen struck at us with one of her claws. Sayrah and I both ducked, but Sayrah wasn't fast enough, and the claw nicked the side of her head. "Shoot it!" Sayrah ordered as we crouched on the ground, trying to avoid the claws. The male beasts stormed toward us from the other side of the room. The disorientation from the light must have worn off.

I aimed the gun at the queen and pulled the trigger multiple times, hearing the familiar swish sound over and over.

None of my shots slowed her down. I kept shooting, hitting her all over, but nothing was working. She slowly made her way down from the ceiling to where we were kneeling on the floor. The other monsters growled. They were right around the corner. I continued shooting at the queen, but nothing was stopping her. Her skin must have some kind of armor.

I realized, at that moment, I was going to die. Everything slowed down. The only thing I could think to do was hold Tierly. I turned as quickly as I could, but while I was turning, someone yanked me down so that I was lying on the ground. I fell onto my shoulder and looked up to see what I thought was an angel.

Sayrah was the one who had pulled me, but Tierly was standing beside us, and she was glowing. A sky-blue aura surrounded her. She stood with her hands at her side, her eyes closed. She was floating about six inches off the ground. I couldn't take my eyes off her even though death awaited me from above. Tierly clasped her hands together, and the light disappeared from around her and relocated to just her hands. She quickly opened her eyes, and the light turned into a blue glowing sword shape. She lifted it up, and just as the queen made it closer to us, Tierly struck her right through her long neck, removing her head. Her whole spiked body fell to the ground in front of us.

The three other aliens had appeared while everything happening, but as soon as the queen's head was off and she was dead, they all stopped coming after us. They stood there for a moment until all three fell to the ground. Then all of the cocoons stopped breathing and started to turn black. Steam rose off them, and they concaved into themselves. That was it. Tierly had killed the queen, and the whole species was dying.

Tierly unclasped her hands, and she slowly floated back to the ground. The glow was gone, and I noticed she was bleeding from her head.

I stood up and looked at her. "Are you okay?" I asked.

"Yes," she said while she looked at me. "I'll be fine. Just have to sit in the immersion tub again," she said with a smile.

Sayrah stood up and looked at me. "Thank you for coming to save us," she said. "Although we were fine. I could have taken them," she said with a wink. That was the nicest Sayrah had ever been to me. Maybe she didn't hate me anymore or, at least, hated me a little less.

"Let's go back to our ship," Tierly said. "This one is about to rot away."

As she said that, I suddenly felt the familiar rush of cool. Once again, I closed my eyes. I wasn't sure if I couldn't look because I was scared or if the cold air just made me panic even more. But almost as quickly as the icy air surrounded me, it was gone. I opened my eyes, and we were back in the teleportation bay.

Tierly, Sayrah, and I all walked back through the passageway to the control room. Talents was standing by the door, and as soon as he saw us, he gave me a tight hug. I was taken aback and stood still with my arms out for a second.

Talents whispered, "Thank you."

I smiled, relaxed, and hugged him back. I hadn't really done anything. The more I thought about it, the more I believed they might have been fine without me. But I appreciated the gesture.

Talents let me go and then jumped on Tierly and Sayrah, who hadn't even made it all the way into the room. He hugged them tightly and said, "I love you both." They stayed in a hugging position for a good minute. A few tears fell from their eyes.

"We're finally free," Tierly whispered as she broke the embrace between her, Sayrah, and Talents. They all smiled at each other.

I stepped farther into the room and stared out the large window at the star-shaped ship that floated lifelessly through the atmosphere. Tierly came up behind me and rested her chin on my shoulder.

“So,” I said as I looked at her, “what do we do now?”

She smiled, lifted her head, and grabbed my hand. “You asked me that same question when Earth was destroyed,” she said. “Do you remember what I told you?”

I looked at her lovingly and smiled. “You told me to live,” I said as I held firmly to her hand.

“Then live we shall,” she said as we both turned our heads to look out the window into the vast universe that I had yet to explore. That was the true beginning of my life. And as I stood next to Tierly, I couldn’t have been any happier to spend it with her.